It has been ten years since Evan Hunter burst upon the literary scene with his first book, *The Blackboard Jungle*. That best-selling novel, with its important sociological implications, established Hunter immediately as a most exciting topical writer. In the ensuing decade his reputation has grown enormously and become solidified as a result of five other major novels, the most recent of which are *Mothers and Daughters* and *Buddwing*.

During the same period, Hunter wrote a number of short stories for magazine publication. This collection presents the best of them and displays the stunning range of the author's interests and talents. There are gay stories and grim stories; realistic stories and wildly fantastic stories; stories of action. Only one thing about the collection is uniform: the intense quality that Hunter puts into everything he writes, which holds the reader spellbound to the page.

Evan Hunter fans will find the two very long stories in the volume of particular interest, for each is a substantial work on its own and represents the author at top form. These are the title story, *Happy New Year, Herbie,* and *Uncle Jimbo's Marbles.*

Books by Evan Hunter

The Blackboard Jungle
Second Ending
Strangers When We Meet
A Matter of Conviction
The Last Spin
Mothers and Daughters
Buddwing

HAPPY NEW YEAR, HERBIE

and other stories by

Evan Hunter

CONSTABLE
LONDON

First published 1965 by
Constable and Company Limited
10–12 Orange Street, London WC2

COPYRIGHT © 1965 BY EVAN HUNTER

Printed in Great Britain by
Western Printing Services Ltd, Bristol

this is for
Peter Schwed

CONTENTS

Here is the man with three staves, and here the Wheel,
And here is the one-eyed merchant, and this card,
Which is blank, is something he carries on his back,
Which I am forbidden to see. I do not find
The Hanged Man. Fear death by water.
I see crowds of people, walking round in a ring.
Thank you. If you see dear Mrs. Equitone,
Tell her I bring the horoscope myself:
One must be so careful these days.

—T. S. ELIOT

UNCLE JIMBO'S MARBLES

LAST SUMMER they quarantined the camp two weeks after we'd arrived.

Uncle Marvin called all us counselors into the dining room one July night and announced briefly that there was a polio scare at a nearby camp. He went on to say that whereas all of *our* campers had of course been vaccinated, he nonetheless felt it would be in the best interests of public safety if we voluntarily agreed not to leave the campgrounds until the threat had subsided. The words "public safety" were Uncle Marvin's own. He was the principal of a junior high school in the Bronx, and he also happened to own Camp Marvin, which is why it was called Camp Marvin and not Camp Chippewa or Mane-toga or Hiawatha. He could have called it "Camp Levine," I suppose, Levine being his last name, but I somehow feel his choice was judicious. Besides, the name Marvin seemed to fit a camp whose owner was a man given to saying things like "public safety," especially when he became *Uncle* Marvin for the summer.

I was Uncle Don for the summer.

The kids in my bunk had never heard of Uncle Don on the radio, so they never made any jokes about my name. To tell the truth, I'd barely heard of him myself. Besides, they were a nice bunch of kids, and we were getting along fine until the voluntary quarantine in the best interests of public safety was declared by Marvin, and then things got a little strained and eventually led to a sort of hysteria.

Marvin's wife was named Lydia, and so the girls' camp across the lake from Camp Marvin was called Camp

11

Lydia, and the entire complex was called Camp Lydia-Marvin, which was possibly one of the most exciting names in the annals of American camp history. I was Uncle Don last summer, and I was nineteen years old. Across the lake in Camp Lydia was a girl named Aunt Rebecca, who was also nineteen years old and whom I loved ferociously. When the quarantine began, I started writing notes to her, and I would have them smuggled across the lake, tied to the handles of the big milk cans. *I love you, Aunt Rebecca,* my notes would say. And I would look across the still waters of the lake and try to imagine Becky opening my note, her dark eyes lowered as she read the words, her quick smile flashing over her face. I imagined she would look up hastily, she moved hastily, her eyes would dart, the smile would widen, she would stare into the distance at the pine trees towering over the boys' cabins, and maybe her heart would skip a beat, and maybe she would murmur softly under her breath, *I love you, too, Uncle Don.*

I hated Camp Marvin.

I will tell you what I loved.

I loved Rebecca Goldblatt, that's all. I had loved Rebecca Goldblatt long before I met her. I had loved her, to tell the truth, from the day I was twelve years old and was allowed to join the adult section of the public library. I had clutched my new card in my hand that bright October day, the card unmarked, every space on it empty, and wandered among the shelves. It was very warm inside the library, warm and hushed, and as I walked past the big windows I could hear the wind outside, and I could see the huge tree out front with its leaves shaking loose every time there was a new gust, and beyond that on the other side of the street some smaller trees, bare already, bending a little in the wind. It was very cold outside, but I was warm as I walked through the aisles with a smile on my face, holding my new library card, and wondering if everyone could tell I was an adult now, it said so on my card.

I found the book on one of the open shelves. The cover was red, tooled in gold. The title was *Ivanhoe*.

And that night I fell in love with Rebecca, not Rebecca Goldblatt, but the girl in *Ivanhoe*. And then when they re-released the movie, I fell in love with her all over again, not Elizabeth Taylor, but Rebecca, the girl in *Ivanhoe*. I can still remember one of the lines in the movie. It had nothing to do with either Ivanhoe's Rebecca or my own Rebecca Goldblatt, but I will never forget it anyway. It was when Robert Taylor was standing horseless, without a shield, trying to fend off the mace blows of the mounted Norman knight. And the judge or the referee, or whatever he was called in those days, looked at Robert Taylor, who had almost hit the Norman's horse with his sword, and shouted, "Beware, Saxon, lest you strike horse!" That was a rule, you see. You weren't allowed to strike the horse.

Oh, how I loved Rebecca Goldblatt!

I loved everything about her, her eyes, her nose, her mouth, her eyes. Her eyes were black. I know a lot of girls claim to have really black eyes, but Rebecca is the only person I have ever known in my entire life whose eyes were truly black and not simply a very dark brown. Sometimes, when she was in a sulky, brooding mood, her eyes got so mysterious and menacing they scared me half to death. Girls' eyes always do that to me when they're in that very dramatic solitary mood, as if they're pondering all the female secrets of the world. But usually her eyes were very bright and glowing, like a black purey. I shouldn't talk about marbles, I suppose, since marbles started all the trouble that summer—but that was how her eyes looked, the way a black purey looks when you hold it up to the sun.

I loved her eyes and I loved her smile, which was fast and open and yet somehow secretive, as if she'd been amused by something for a very long time before allowing it to burst onto her mouth. And I loved her figure which was very slender with sort of small breasts and very long legs that carried her in a strange sort of lope, especially when she was wearing a trenchcoat, don't ask me why. I loved her name and the way she looked. I loved her walk, and I loved the way she talked, too, a sort of combination of middle-class Bronx Jewish girl with a touch of City College Speech One thrown in, which is where she went to school and which is where I met her.

I think I should tell you now that I'm Italian.

That's how I happened to be at Camp Marvin in Stockbridge, Massachusetts, with a girl named Rebecca Goldblatt across the lake in Camp Lydia.

I know that's not much of a problem these days, what with new nations clamoring for freedom, and Federal troops crawling all over the South, and discrimination of all sorts every place you look. It's not much of a problem unless you happen to be nineteen years old and involved in it, and then it seems like a pretty big problem. I'm too young to have seen *Abie's Irish Rose,* but I honestly don't think I will ever understand what was so funny about *that* situation, believe me. I didn't think it was so funny last summer, and I still don't think it's funny, but maybe what happened with Uncle Jimbo's marbles had something to do with that. I don't really know. I just know for certain now that you can get so involved in something you don't really see the truth of it any more. And the simple truth of Becky and me was that we loved each other. The rest of it was all hysteria, like with the marbles.

I have to tell you that I didn't want to go to Camp Marvin in the first place. It was all Becky's idea, and she presented it with that straightforward solemn look she always gets on her face when she discusses things like sending food to the starving people in China or disarmament or thalidomide or pesticides. She gets so deep and so involved sometimes that I feel like kissing her. Anyway, it was her idea, and I didn't like it because I said it sounded to me like hiding.

"It's not hiding," Becky said.

"Then what is it if not hiding?" I answered. "I don't *want* to be a counselor this summer. I want to go to the beach and listen to records and hold your hand."

"They have a beach at Camp Marvin," Becky said.

"And I don't like the name of the camp."

"Why not?"

"It's unimaginative. Anybody who would name a place Camp Marvin must be a very unimaginative person."

"He's a junior high school principal," Becky said.

"That only proves my point." She was looking very very solemn just about then, the way she gets when we discuss the Cuban situation, so I said, "Give me one good reason why we should go to Stockbridge, Massachusetts, to a camp named *Marvin*, of all things, would you please?"

"Yes."

"Well, go ahead."

"We would be together all summer," Becky said simply, "and we wouldn't have to hide from my father."

"That's the craziest thing I ever heard in my life," I

said. "You want to go away and hide from him just so we won't have to hide from him."

"That's not what I'm saying," Becky said.

"Then what is it, if not hiding from him?"

"It's not my fault he's a bigoted jerk!" Becky said angrily, and I didn't realize how much this meant to her until that minute, because tears suddenly sprang into her eyes. I never know what to do when a girl starts crying, especially someone you love.

"Becky," I said, "if we run away this summer, we're only confirming his . . ."

"He doesn't even know you, Donald," she said. "He doesn't know how sweet you are."

"Yes, but if we hide from him . . ."

"If he'd only meet you, if he'd only talk to you . . ."

"Yes, but if we run away to hide, then all we're doing is joining in with his lunacy, honey. Can't you see that?"

"My father is not a lunatic," Becky said. "My father is a dentist and a prejudiced ass, but he's not a lunatic. And anyway, you have to remember that *his* father can still remember pogroms in Russia."

"All right, but this isn't Russia," I said.

"I know."

"And I'm not about to ride into the town and rape all the women and kill all the men."

"You don't even know *how* to ride," Becky said.

"That's right," I said, "but even if I *did* know how to ride, I wouldn't do it."

"I know, you're so sweet," Becky said.

"Okay. Now if your father believes that I'm some kind of assassin with a stiletto, that's *his* fantasy, you see, Beck? And if I sneak away with you this summer, then I'm *joining* his fantasy, I'm becoming as crazy as he is. How can you ask me to do that?"

"I can ask you because I love you and I want to be alone with you without having to sneak and skulk all the time. It isn't fair."

"What isn't fair?"

"Sneaking and skulking all the time."

"That's right."

"When I love you so much."

"I love you, too, Beck," I said. "But . . ."

"Well, if you love me so much, it seems like a very simple thing to do to simply say you'll come with me to Camp Lydia-Marvin this summer."

I didn't say anything.

"Donald?" Becky said.

"This is a mistake," I said, shaking my head.

"We'll be alone."

"We'll be surrounded by eight thousand screaming kids!"

"The kids go to sleep early."

"We'll be hiding, we'll be—"

"We'll be alone."

"Damn it, Becky, sometimes . . ."

"Will you come, Donald?"

"Well, what else can I do? Let you go alone?"

"I think that's what scares my father," Becky said, the smile coming onto her mouth, her black eyes glowing.

"What are you talking about?"

"That fiery Italian temper."

"Yeah, go to hell, you *and* your father," I said smiling, and then I kissed her because what else can you do with a girl like that whom you love so terribly much?

That's how we came to be at Camp Lydia-Marvin last summer.

The quarantine was very ironic in an O. Henry way because we had gone to camp to be *together,* you see, and when Uncle Marvin had his bright quarantine idea, he really meant *quarantine,* the girls with the girls and the boys with the boys. So there was Rebecca clear the hell over on the other side of the lake, and here was I with a bunch of counselors named Uncle Bud and Uncle Jimbo and Uncle Dave and Uncle Ronnie and even Uncle Emil, who was a gym teacher at Benjamin Franklin High School in Manhattan. All the uncles took the quarantine in high good spirits for the first week, I guess. I must admit that even I found a sense of adventure in tying my love notes to the handles of the milk cans. I never once questioned the validity of a quarantine that allowed milk to be passed from one side of the lake to the other. In fact, if it hadn't been for the milk cans, I would have gone out of my mind immediately. As it was, I *almost* went out of my mind, but not until much later. And by that time everybody was a little nutty.

I think it all started with the kids. Everything usually starts with kids. I once read a Ray Bradbury story called "Invasion" or something, about these Martians, or aliens, anyway, I don't remember which planet, who are planning an invasion of Earth, and they're doing it through the kids. Boy, that story scared me, I can tell you, since I have a kid brother who gets a very fanatical gleam in his eye every now and then. I wouldn't be at all surprised.

The thing that started with the kids was the marbles. Now every kid who goes to camp for the summer takes marbles with him. There's usually what they call Free Play or Unassigned, and that's when the kids go to ping-pong or tether ball or marbles. Marbles were very big at

Camp Marvin, especially after the quarantine started, though I'm still not sure whether the quarantine really had anything to do with the craze. Maybe there was just an unusual number of marbles at camp that summer, I don't know. At the end there, it sure *seemed* like a lot of marbles. The most marbles I had ever seen in my life before that was when I was eight years old and still living in Manhattan, before we moved up to the Bronx. My mother and father gave me a *hundred* marbles for my birthday, and they also gave me a leather pouch with drawstrings to put the marbles in. I went downstairs with the hundred marbles, and I lost them all in a two-hour game. I almost lost the pouch, too, because a kid on the block wanted to trade me forty immies and a steelie for it, but I had the wisdom to refuse the offer. I'll never forget my mother's face when I went upstairs and told her I'd been wiped out.

"You lost *all* the marbles?" she asked incredulously.

"Yeah, all the immies," I said.

"How?"

"Just playing immies," I said.

They didn't play immies at Camp Marvin; they played marbles. They used to draw a circle in the dirt, and each kid would put five or six marbles in the circle and try to hit them out with his shooter. I didn't know how to play marbles because all I played as a kid was immies, which is played by the curb, in the gutter. In fact, it was best to play immies after a rainstorm because then there would be puddles all over the street, and you never knew where the other guy's immie was. You just shot and prayed and felt around in the dirty water with your hand spread, trying to span the immies. It used to be fun when I was a kid. A city street is something like a summer camp all year round, you see. There are always a thousand kids on the block and a hundred games to choose from: stickball, stoopball, skullies, Johnny-on-a-Pony, Kick the Can, Statues, Salugi, Ring-a-Leavio, hundreds of games. I sometimes wonder why the *Herald Tribune* sends slum kids to the country. I think somebody ought to start sending country kids to the slums. In a way, when the marble craze started at Camp Marvin, it was very much like a craze starting on a city street, where one day a kid will come down with his roller skates, and the next day the roller-skating season has started. It was the same thing with the marbles at Camp Marvin. A couple of kids started a game, and before any of us were really completely aware of it, there were marble games being played all over the camp.

It would have been all right if the craze had restricted itself to the kids. But you have to remember that we were quarantined, which meant that we worked with the kids all day long, and then were not permitted to leave the grounds at night, on our time off. Children are very nice and all that, and someday I hope to have a dozen of my own, but that summer it was important to get away from them every now and then. I mean, physically and geographically *away* from them. It was important to have other interests. It was important to have an emotional and mental respite. What it was important to do, in fact, was to hold Becky in my arms and kiss her, but Marvin of course had made that impossible with his stupid quarantine. The funny thing was he didn't seem to miss his wife Lydia at all. Maybe that's because they'd been married for fourteen years. But most of the rest of us began to feel the strain of the quarantine by the end of the second week, and I think it was then that Uncle Jimbo ventured into his first game of marbles.

Jimbo, like the rest of us, was beginning to crave a little action. He was a very tall man who taught science at a high school someplace in Brooklyn. His real name was James McFarland, but in the family structure of Camp Marvin he immediately became Uncle Jim. And then, because it is fatal to have a name like Jim at any camp, he was naturally renamed Jimbo. He seemed like a very serious fellow, this Jimbo, about thirty-eight years old, with a wife and two kids at home. He wore eyeglasses, and he had sandy-colored hair that was always falling onto his forehead. The forehead itself bore a perpetual frown, even when he was playing marbles, as if he were constantly trying to figure out one of Einstein's theories. He always wore sneakers and Bermuda shorts that had been made by cutting down a pair of dungarees. When the quarantine started, one of the kids in his bunk painted a big PW on Jimbo's dungaree Bermuda shorts, the PW standing for prisoner of war—a joke Jimbo didn't think was very comical. I knew how he felt. I wasn't married, of course, but I knew what it was like to be separated from someone you loved, and Jimbo's wife and kids were away the hell out there in Brooklyn while we were locked up in Stockbridge.

I happened to be there the day he joined one of the games, thereby starting the madness that followed. He had found a single marble near the tennis courts and then had gone foraging on his free time until he'd come up with half a dozen more. It was just after dinner, and three kids were playing in front of my bunk when Jimbo strolled over and asked if he could get in the game. If there's one thing a kid can spot at fifty paces, it's a sucker. They took one look at the tall science teacher from Brooklyn and fairly leaped on him in their anxiety to get him in the

game. Well, that was the last leaping any of them did for
the rest of the evening. Jimbo had seven marbles. He put
six of them in the ring, and he kept the biggest one for his
shooter. The kids, bowing graciously to their guest,
allowed him to shoot first. Standing ten feet from the
circle in the dust, Jimbo took careful aim and let his
shooter go. It sprang out of his hand with the speed of
sound, almost cracking a marble in the dead center of the
ring and sending it flying out onto the surrounding
dirt.

The kids weren't terribly impressed because they were
very hip and knew all about beginner's luck. They didn't
begin to realize they were playing with a pro until they
saw Jimbo squat down on one knee and proceed to knock
every single marble out of the ring without missing a shot.
Then, because there's no sucker like a sucker who thinks
he knows one, the kids decided they could take Jimbo
anyway, and they spent the rest of the evening disprov-
ing the theory by losing marble after marble to him.
Jimbo told me later that he'd been raised in Plainfield,
New Jersey, and had played marbles practically every day
of his childhood. But the kids didn't know that at the time,
and by the end of that first evening Jimbo had won perhaps two hundred marbles.

I wasn't sure I liked what Jimbo had done. He was,
after all, a grown man, and he was playing with kids, and
one of the kids he'd beaten happened to be a kid in my
bunk. I watched that kid walk away from the game after
Jimbo had collected all the marbles. His name was Max,
which is a funny name for a kid anyway, and he was walking with his head bent, his hands in the pockets of his
shorts, his sneakers scuffing the ground.

"What's the matter, Max?" I asked.

"Nothing," he said.

"Come here, sit down," I said. He came over and sat on the bunk steps with me. I knew better than to talk about the marbles he had lost. I talked about the baseball game that afternoon and about the volleyball tournament, and all the while I was thinking of those hundred marbles I had got for my eighth birthday, and the leather pouch, and the look on my mother's face when I climbed to the third floor and told her I'd lost them all. It was getting on about dusk, and I said to Max, "Something very important is going to happen in just a few minutes, Max. Do you know what it is?"

"No," Max said.

"Well, can you guess?"

"I don't know. Is it the boxing matches tonight?" he asked.

"No, this is before the boxing matches."

"Well, what is it?" he asked.

"It happens every day at about this time," I said, "and we hardly ever stop to look at it." Max turned his puzzled face up to mine. "Look out there, Max," I said. "Look out there over the lake."

Together, Max and I sat and serenely watched the sunset.

The madness started the next day.

It started when Uncle Emil, the gym teacher from Benjamin Franklin, decided that marbles was essentially a game of athletic skill. Being a gym teacher and also being in charge of the camp's entire sports program, he naturally decided that in order to uphold his honor and his title, he would have to defeat Uncle Jimbo. He didn't declare a formal match or anything like that. He simply wandered up to Jimbo during the noon rest hour and said, "Hey, Jimbo, want to shoot some marbles?"

Jimbo looked at him with the slow steady gaze of a renowned gunslick and then said, "Sure. Why not?" Lazily he went back to his own bunk. In a few minutes he returned with a cigar box containing his winnings of the night before. They drew a circle in the dust, and each put twelve marbles in the circle. I was only sitting there writing a letter to Becky, and I guess they decided I wasn't doing anything important, so they made me referee. Jimbo was wearing a yellow short-sleeved sports shirt and his sawed-off dungarees. Emil was wearing spotless white shorts and a spotless white T shirt, as if he were about to settle the Davis Cup at Wimbledon or someplace. They flipped a coin to see who would shoot first. Emil won the toss.

Standing behind the line they had drawn in the dust some ten feet from the ring, Emil held his shooter out and sighted along the length of his arm. Jimbo stood watching him with a faintly amused look on his face. I looked up from my letter because I was supposed to be referee, even though I'd been in the middle of telling Becky I loved her, which I always seemed to be in the middle of doing whenever I got the chance. Emil licked his lips with his tongue, cocked his thumb against the big marble in his fist, and then triggered his shot. The marble leaped from his hand, spinning across the open air in a direct, unwavering, deadly accurate line toward the middle of the circle. It collided with one of the marbles in the ring, which richocheted off onto another marble, which struck two more marbles, which knocked out yet another marble for a total of five marbles knocked out of the circle on the first shot. I must admit I felt a slight thrill of pleasure. I can remember thinking, *All right, Jimbo, this time you're not playing with kids.* But I can also remember looking over at Jimbo and noticing that he didn't seem at all disturbed, that he was still wearing that same faintly amused expression on his long face.

Emil walked to the ring and, grinning, turned to Jimbo and said, "Want to forfeit?"

"Shoot," Jimbo said.

Emil grinned again, crouched in the dust, picked up his big marble, and shot. He knocked two more marbles out of the ring in succession and then missed the third by a hair, and that was the end of the game. I say that was the end of the game only because Jimbo then shot and knocked out all the remaining marbles in the circle. And then, because he had won this round, it was his turn to shoot first in the next round. He shot first, and he knocked four marbles out with his opening blast, and then proceeded to clean up the ring again. And then, because he'd won this round as well, he shot first again, and again cleaned up the ring, and he kept doing that all through the rest period until he'd won seventy-five marbles from Uncle Emil.

Uncle Emil muttered something about having a little rheumatism in his fingers, throwing his game off, and Jimbo listened sympathetically while he added the seventy-five marbles to the collection in his bulging cigar box. That afternoon Emil came back with a hundred marbles he had scrounged from the kids, and Jimbo won them all in a matter of a half hour. That evening Jimbo went to the mess hall to pick up a cardboard carton for his marble winnings. And, also that evening, he became a celebrity.

I guess I was the only person, man or boy, in that camp

who didn't want to try beating Uncle Jimbo in the hectic weeks that followed. To begin with, I am not a very competitive fellow, and besides, I only knew how to play immies, not marbles. Marbles required a strong thumb and a fast eye, Jimbo explained to me. My thumbs were pretty weak and my eyes were tired from staring across the lake trying to catch a glimpse of a distant figure I could identify as Becky. But everyone else in camp seemed to possess powerful thumbs and 20/20 vision, and they were all anxious to pit these assets against the champion. When you come to think of it, I suppose, champions exist *only* to be challenged, anyway. The challengers in this case included *everybody,* and all for different reasons.

Uncle Ronnie was a counselor whom everyone, including the kids, called Horizontal Ronnie because his two favorite pursuits both required a bed and a horizontal position. He wanted to beat Jimbo because the quarantine had deprived him of the satisfying company of a girl named Laura in Camp Lydia. Jimbo won two hundred marbles from Ronnie in an hour of play.

Uncle Dave taught mathematics at Evander Childs High School, and he thought he had figured out a foolproof system that he wanted to try in practice. The system worked for fifteen minutes, at the end of which time Jimbo blasted the game from its hinges and then barged on through to win a hundred and fifty marbles.

Uncle Marvin, too, had his own reason for wanting to beat Jimbo. Before the season had begun, when Marvin was still hiring counselors, he had offered Jimbo twelve hundred dollars for the job. Jimbo had held out for thirteen hundred, which Marvin eventually and grudgingly paid him. But the extra hundred dollars rankled, and Marvin was determined to get it back somehow.

You may think it odd that he decided to get back his hundred dollars by winning *marbles* from Jimbo. After all, marbles are marbles, and money is money. But a very strange thing had happened in the second week of the madness. Marbles, which up to that time had only been round pieces of colored glass, suddenly became the hottest item of currency in the camp's vast and complicated trading system. Before then, dimes were very hot property because the Coke machine in the counselors' shack took only dimes. The kids weren't allowed to enter the counselors' shack, nor were they allowed to drink Cokes, all of which made it absolutely necessary for them to have dimes so they could sneak into the counselors' shack and drink Cokes. Almost every letter home, before the marble madness began, started with the words, "Dear Mom and Dad, I am fine. Please send me some dimes." But suddenly, because Jimbo kept winning marbles with such frequency, there was a shortage of marbles in the camp. Marbles became a precious commodity, like gold or silver, and the basis of the camp economy. If you had marbles, you could trade them for all the dimes you needed. You could, in fact, get almost anything you wanted, if you only had marbles. Uncle Jimbo had a lot of marbles. Uncle Jimbo had a whole damn suitcase full of them, which he kept locked and on a shelf over his bed. He was surely the richest man in camp.

He became even richer the afternoon he played Uncle Marvin and won five hundred marbles from him, a blow from which Marvin never recovered. By this time, beating Jimbo had become an obsession. Jimbo was the sole topic of camp discussion, overshadowing the approaching Color War, eclipsing the visit of a famous football player who talked about the ways and means of forward passing while nobody listened. The counselors, the kids, even the camp doctor, were interested only in the ways and means of amassing more marbles to pit against Jimbo's growing empire. They discussed shooting techniques, and whether or not they should play with the sun facing them or behind their backs. They discussed the potency of the mass shot as against a slow deliberate one-at-a-time sort of game. They discussed different kinds of shooters, the illegality of using steelies, the current exchange rate of pureys. The kids loved every minute of it. They awoke each morning brimming with plans for Jimbo's ultimate downfall. To them, beating him was important only because it would give them an opportunity to prove that adults, especially adult counselors, were all a bunch of no-good finks.

On Monday of the third week of the madness, the smart money entered the marbles business—and the gambling element began taking over.

But before that, on Sunday night, I broke quarantine.

I am usually a law-abiding fellow, and I might never have broken quarantine were it not for Horizontal Ronnie, who, I later came to learn, had very definite criminal leanings.

"Look," he said to me, "what's to stop us from taking one of the canoes and paddling over to the other side?"

"Well," I said, "there's a polio scare."

"Don't you want to see What's-her-name?"

"Rebecca."

"Yeah, don't you want to see her?"

"Sure I do."

"Has every kid in this camp and also in Camp Lydia, by Marvin's own admission, in his very own words, been inoculated against polio?"

"Well, yes," I said.

"Then would you mind telling me how there is a polio scare?"

"I don't know," I said.

"Fine. I'll meet you at the boat dock tonight at nine o'clock. I'll take care of getting word to the girls."

I guess I didn't trust him even then, because I took care of getting word to Becky myself that afternoon, by sending over one of my notes tied to an empty milk can. That night, at nine o'clock on the dot, Ronnie and I met at the boat dock and silently slipped one of the canoes into the water. We didn't talk at all until we were in the middle of the lake, and then Ronnie said, "We'll come back around eleven. Is that all right with you?"

"Sure," I said.

"Boy, that Laura," he said, and fell silent again, apparently contemplating what was ahead. Laura, whom I had only seen once or twice before the quarantine, was a very pretty blond girl who always wore white sweaters and tight white shorts. She also wore a perfume that was very hard to avoid smelling, and the few times I had seen her was in the counselors' shack where she kept playing the "Malaguena" over and over again on the piano. She was a very mysterious girl, what with her sweater and shorts and her perfume and her "Malaguena." She was eighteen years old.

"I think I know how to beat him," Ronnie said suddenly.

"Huh?"

"Jimbo. I think I know how to beat the bastard."

"How?" I asked.

"Never mind," Ronnie said, and then he fell silent again, but it seemed to me he was paddling more furiously.

I met Rebecca under the pines bordering the lake. She was wearing black slacks and a black bulky sweater, and she rushed into my arms and didn't say anything for the longest time, just held herself close to me, and then lifted her head and stared into my face, and then smiled that fast-breaking smile, and fleetingly kissed me on the cheek, and pulled away and looked into my face again.

We skirted the edge of the pine forest, the night was still, I could feel her hand tight in my own. We sat with our backs to one of the huge boulders overlooking the lake, and I held her in my arms and told her how miserable I'd been without her, and she kept kissing my closed eyes as I spoke, tiny little punctuating kisses that made me weak.

The night was very dark. Somewhere across the lake a dog began barking, and then the barking stopped and the night was still again.

"I can barely see you, Becky," I whispered.

I held her close, I held her slender body close to mine. She was Becky, she was trembling, she was joy and sadness together, echoing inside me. If I held her a moment longer my heart would burst, I knew my heart would burst and shower trailing sparks on the night. And yet I held her, wanting to cry in my happiness, dizzy with the smell of her hair, loving everything about her in that timeless, brimming moment, still knowing my heart would burst, loving her closed eyes and the whispery touch of her lashes, and the rough wool of her sweater, and the delicate motion of her hands on my face. I kissed her, I died, I smiled, I listened to thunder, for oh, the kiss of Rebecca Goldblatt, the kiss, the heart-stopping kiss of my girl.

The world was dark and still.

"I love you," she said.

"I love you," I said.

And then she threw her arms around my neck and put her face against mine, tight, I could feel her cheekbone hard against mine, and suddenly she was crying.

"Hey," I said. "What . . . honey, what is it?"

"Oh, Donald," she said, "what are we going to do? I love you so much."

"I think we ought to tell him," I said, "when we get back."

"How can we do that?" Becky said.

"I can go to him. I can say we're in love with each other."

"Oh yes, *yes*," Becky said breathlessly. "I *do* love you, Donald."

"Then that's what we'll do."

"He . . ." She shook her head in the darkness. I knew that her eyes were very solemn, even though I couldn't see them. "He won't listen," Becky said. "He'll try to break us up."

"Nobody will ever break us up," I said. "Ever."

"What—what will you tell him?"

"That we love each other. That when we finish school we're going to get married."

"He won't let us."

"The hell with him."

"He doesn't *know* you. He thinks Italians are terrible."

"I can't help what he thinks," I said.

"Donald . . ." She paused. She was shaking her head again, and she began to tremble. "Donald, you can't do it."

"Why not?"

"Because he *believes* it, don't you see? He really believes you *are* some—some terrible sort of person."

"I know, but that doesn't make it true. And simply

because *he* believes it is no reason for me to behave as if *I* believe it." I nodded my head in the darkness. I felt pretty convinced by what I was saying, but at the same time I was scared to death of facing her father. "I'll tell him when we get back," I said.

Becky was quiet for a long time.

Then she said, "If only I was Italian."

I held her very close to me, and I kissed the top of her head very gently. Right then I knew everything was going to be all right. I knew it because Becky had said, "If only I was Italian," when she could just as easily have said, "If only you were Jewish."

Horizontal Ronnie swung into action the very next day.

He had been inordinately silent the night before on the trip back across the lake, and I hadn't disturbed his thoughts because I assumed he was working out his system for beating Jimbo. Besides, I was working out what I would tell Becky's father when we got back to the city.

The course of action Ronnie decided upon was really the only one that offered the slightest opportunity of defeating Jimbo and destroying his empire. He had correctly concluded that Jimbo was the best marble player in camp, if not in the entire world, and had further reasoned it would be impossible to beat him through skill alone. So, discounting skill, Ronnie had decided to try his hand at luck. At eight o'clock that Monday morning, as the kids lined up for muster, Ronnie came over with his fist clenched. He held out his hand to one of the senior boys and said, "Odds or evens?"

"Huh?" the senior said. The senior boys at Camp Marvin weren't exactly the brightest kids in the world. In fact, the junior boys had written a song about them which went something like "We've got seen-yuh boys, dumpy, lumpy seen-yuh boys, we've got seen-yuh boys, the worst!" Besides, it was only eight o'clock in the morning, and when someone thrusts his fist in your face at eight o'clock in the morning and says, "Odds or evens?" what else can you reply but "Huh?"

"My fist is full of marbles," Ronnie explained.

"Yeah?" the senior boy said. Mention of marbles seemed to have awakened him suddenly. His eyes gleamed.

"They're either an odd number of marbles or an even number," Ronnie went on. "You guess odds or evens. If you're right, I give you the marbles in my hand. If you're wrong, you match the marbles in my hand."

"You mean if I'm wrong I give you the number of marbles you're holding?"

"That's right."

The senior boy thought this over carefully for a moment, then nodded and said, "Odds."

Ronnie opened his fist. There were four marbles in his hand.

"You pay me," he said, and that was the beginning of the Las Vegas phase of the marble madness.

If Uncle Marvin saw what was going on, he made no comment upon it. The common opinion was that he was still smarting from his loss of five hundred marbles to Jimbo and deliberately avoided contact with everyone in the camp. It is doubtful that he could have stopped the frenzy even if he'd wanted to. The kids, presented with a new and exciting activity, took to it immediately. Here was a sport that required no skill. Here was a game that promised and delivered immediate action: the closed fist, the simple question, the guess, the payoff. Kids who were hopeless washouts on the baseball diamond suddenly discovered a sport in which they could excel. Kids who couldn't sing a note in a camp musical set the grounds reverberating with their shouted "Odds or evens?" A large shipment of marbles from home to a kid named Irwin in bunk nine only increased the feverish tempo of the gambling activity. The simple guessing game started at reveille each morning, before a kid's feet had barely touched the wooden floor of his bunk. It did not end until lights out, and even after that there were the whispered familiar words, and the surreptitious glow of flashlights.

Uncle Jimbo, startled by this new development, stayed fastidiously away from the gambling in the first few days. Ronnie, meanwhile, exhibiting his true gambler's instincts, began by slowly winning a handful of marbles from every kid he could challenge, and then became more and more reckless with his bets, clenching his fists around as many marbles as they could hold. Before too long, a bookie system became necessary, with counselors and campers writing down a number on a slip of paper and then folding the slip, so that a challenger had only to guess odds or evens on a written figure rather than on an actual fistful of marbles. That week, Ronnie successfully and infallibly called bets ranging from a low of three marbles to a high of a hundred and fifty-two marbles. It became clear almost immediately that if Jimbo were to defend his title, he would have to enter this new phase of the sport or lose by default.

I think he was beginning to like his title by then. Or perhaps he was only beginning to like his wealth. Whatever it was, he could not afford to drop out of the race. He studied the new rules, and learned them. They were really quite simple. If someone challenged you, you could either accept or decline the challenge. But once you had accepted, once the question "Odds or evens?" was asked in earnest, you either called immediately or lost the bet by default. In the beginning, Jimbo took no chances. He deliberately sought out only those campers whose luck had been running incredibly bad. His bets were small, four marbles, seven marbles, a dozen marbles. If he won a bet, he immediately pocketed a portion of his initial investment and then began playing on his winnings alone. And then, because he thought of himself as a blood-smelling champion closing in for the kill, he began to bet more heavily, taking on all comers, swinging freely through the camp, challenging campers and counselors alike. Eventually he wrote a bookie slip for five hundred and seven marbles and won the bet from a kid in bunk seven, knocking him completely out of the competition. Jimbo's luck was turning out to be almost as incredible as his skill had been. He lost occasionally, oh yes, but his winnings kept mounting, and marble after marble poured into the locked suitcase on the shelf over his bed. It was becoming apparent to almost everyone in the camp—except Uncle Marvin, who still didn't know what the hell was going on—that an elimination match was taking place, and that the chief contenders for Jimbo's as yet unchallenged title were Ronnie and the *nouveau riche* kid in bunk nine, who had parlayed his shipment from home into a sizable fortune.

Irwin, the kid in bunk nine, was a tiny little kid whom everybody called Irwin the Vermin. He wore glasses, and he always had a runny nose and a disposition to match. Ronnie, correctly figuring he would have to collar every loose marble in the camp before a showdown with Jimbo, went over to bunk nine one afternoon and promptly challenged Irwin the Vermin. The number of marbles being wagered on a single bet had by this time reached fairly astronomical proportions. It was rumored that Irwin owned one thousand seven hundred and fifty marbles. Ronnie, whose number of marbles now totaled nine hundred and four, sat on the edge of Irwin's bed and wrote out a slip of paper with the number 903 on it.

He folded the slip of paper and then looked Irwin directly in the eye.

"Odds or evens?" he said.

Irwin blinked behind his glasses, grinned maliciously, licked his lips with his tongue and said, "Odds."

Ronnie swallowed. "What?"

"Odds," Irwin repeated.

"Yeah," Ronnie said. He unfolded the slip, and together they walked back to his bunk where he made payment. "I've got a few marbles left," he lied; he had only one marble to his name. "Do you want to play some more?"

Irwin looked at him steadily and then, true to his nature, said, "Find yourself another sucker, jerk."

Ronnie watched Irwin as he left the bunk loaded down with his winnings. He must have seen in that tiny figure retreating across the grounds a symbol of all his frustration, the quarantine that kept him from the mysterious Laura, the defeat of his system to beat Jimbo. It was late afternoon, and the cries of the boys at Free Play sounded from the ball diamonds and the basketball courts far off in the camp hills. Ronnie must have watched little Irwin walking away with his shattered hopes and dreams in a brown cardboard carton, and it must have been then that he made his final decision, the decision that brought the marble madness to its peak of insanity.

I was coming back from the tennis courts, where I was trying to help little Max with his backhand, when I saw

Ronnie striding across the grounds towards Jimbo's bunk. He was carrying an old battered suitcase, and there was something odd about his walk, a purposeful, angry stride which was at the same time somewhat surreptitious. I looked at him curiously and then followed him past the flagpole and watched as he entered the bunk. I stood outside for a few minutes, wondering, and then I quietly climbed the front steps.

Ronnie was in the middle of forcing the lock on Jimbo's suitcase. He looked up when I entered the bunk and then went right back to work.

"What are you doing?" I said.

"What does it look like I'm doing?" he answered.

"It looks like you're trying to break open Jimbo's suitcase."

"That's right," Ronnie said, and in that moment he broke the lock and opened the lid. "Give me a hand here," he said.

"No."

"Come on, don't be a jerk."

"You're stealing his marbles," I said.

"That's just what I'm doing. It's a gag. Come on, give me a hand here."

The next second was when I almost lost my own sanity because I said, I actually heard myself say, "You can go to jail for that!" as if even *I* had begun to believe there was a fortune in that suitcase instead of hunks of colored glass.

"For stealing marbles?" Ronnie asked incredulously. "Don't be a jackass."

His answer startled me back to reality, but at the same time it puzzled me. Because here he was, a grown man, twenty years old, and he was telling me these were only marbles, and yet he was thoroughly involved in all this frantic nuttiness, so involved that he was in Jimbo's bunk actually *stealing* marbles which he claimed he *knew* were only marbles. He opened his own suitcase and then, seeing I was staring at him with a dumfounded expression, and knowing I wasn't about to help him, he lifted Jimbo's bag himself and tilted it. The marbles spilled from one bag to the other, bright shining marbles, yellow and red and striped and black and green; glass marbles and steelies and glistening pureys, marbles of every size and hue, thousands and thousands of marbles, spilling from Jimbo's bag to Ronnie's in a dazzling, glittering heap.

I shook my head and said, "I think you're all nuts," and then I walked out of the bunk. Ronnie came out after me a minute later, carrying his own full suitcase, bending over with the weight of it. I watched him as he struggled across to the flagpole in the center of the camp. He put the bag down at his feet and then, his eyes gleaming, he cupped his hands to his mouth and shouted, "Where's Jimbo McFarland?"

There was no answer.

"Where's Jimbo McFarland?" he shouted again.

"Stop yelling," I called from the steps of the bunk. "He's up at the handball courts."

"Jimbo McFarland!" Ronnie screamed. "Jimbo McFarland!" and the camp voice-telephone system picked up the name, shouting it across behind the bunks and down by the gully and through the nature shack, "Jimbo McFarland!" and over to the lake where some kids were taking their Red Cross tests, and then up into the hills by the mess hall, and across the upper-camp baseball diamond, and the volleyball court, and finally reaching Jimbo where he was playing handball with one of the counselors.

Jimbo came striding down into the camp proper. He walked out of the hills like the gunslick he was, his back to the sun, crossing the dusty grounds for a final showdown, stopping some twenty feet from where Ronnie stood near the flagpole.

"You calling me?" he said.

"You want to play marbles?" Ronnie answered.

"Have you *got* any marbles?" Jimbo said

"Will you match whatever I've got?"

Jimbo hesitated a moment, weighing his luck, and then said, "Sure," tentatively accepting the challenge.

"Whatever's in this bag?" Ronnie asked.

Again Jimbo hesitated. A crowd of kids had begun to gather, some of whom had followed Jimbo down out of the hills, the rest of whom had felt an excitement in the air, had felt that the moment of truth had finally arrived. They milled around the flagpole, waiting for Jimbo's decision. The gauntlet was in the dust, the challenge had been delivered, and now they waited for the undisputed champion to decide whether or not he would defend his title. Jimbo nodded.

"However much you want to bet," he said slowly, "is all right with me." He had irrevocably accepted the challenge. He now had to call or lose the bet by default.

"Okay, then," Ronnie said. He stooped down beside his suitcase. Slowly, nonchalantly, he unclasped the latches on either side. He put one hand gently on the lid, and then he looked up at Jimbo, grinned, quietly said, "Odds or evens, Jimbo?" and snapped open the lid of the bag.

From where I sat, I saw Jimbo's face go white. I don't know what crossed his mind in those few terrible moments as he stared into the bag at those thousands and thousands of marbles. I don't know whether or not he even made a mental stab at calculating the number of glistening spheres in the suitcase. I only know that he staggered back a pace and his jaw fell slack. The kids were silent now, watching him. Ronnie kept squatting beside the suitcase, his hand resting on the opened lid, the sun glowing on the marbles.

"Well, Jimbo?" he said. "Odds or evens?"

"I . . ."

"Odds or evens, Jimbo?"

Perhaps Jimbo was feverishly calculating in those breathless moments. Perhaps he was realizing he had walked into a trap from which there was no return: he would either call correctly and become the marble king of the entire world; or he would call incorrectly or not at all, and lose his fortune and his fame.

"Odds or evens?" Ronnie demanded.

Odds or evens, but how to call? How many thousands of marbles were in that suitcase, and really what difference did it make when it all narrowed down to a single marble, the real difference between odds and evens, one solitary marble, call wrong and the empire would come crashing down. Jimbo took a deep breath. The sweat was standing out on his face, his eyes were blinking. The kids around the flagpole stood silently awaiting his decision. Ronnie squatted by the suitcase with his hand on the lid.

"Odds or evens?' he asked again.

Jimbo shrugged. Honestly, because it was what he was really thinking, he said, "I . . . I don't know."

"Did you hear him?" Ronnie said immediately. "He loses by default!"

"Wait a minute, I . . ."

"You refused to call, you said you didn't know! I win by default!" Ronnie said, and he snapped the lid of the bag shut, latched it and immediately lifted it from the ground.

"Now just a second," Jimbo protested, but Ronnie was already walking away from him. He stopped some five paces from the flagpole, turned abruptly, put the bag down, grinned, and said, "You stupid jerk! They were your own marbles!"

For a moment, his announcement hung on the dust-laden air. Jimbo blinked, not understanding him at first. The kids were silent and puzzled in the circle around the flagpole. Ronnie picked up the bag of marbles again and began walking toward his bunk with it, a triumphant grin on his face. And then the meaning of what he had said registered on Jimbo's face, his eyes first, intelligence sparking there, his nose next, the nostrils flaring, his mouth then, the lips pulling back to show his teeth, and then his voice, bursting from his mouth in a wounded roar. "You thief!"

His words, too, hung on the silent air, and then one of the kids said, "Did he steal them from you, Uncle Jimbo?" and another kid shouted, "He's a crook!" and then suddenly the word "Thief!" was shouted by one of the senior boys and picked up by a junior, "Thief!" and the air rang with the word, "Thief!" and then it was shouted in unison, "Thief! Thief!' and all at once there was a blood-thirsty mob. A kid who had come down from the ball diamond waved his bat in the air and began running after Ronnie. Another kid seized a fallen branch and rushed past the flagpole with it. The others bellowed screams of anger and rage, hysterically racing toward Ronnie, who had dropped the suitcase and turned to face them. There was a pale, sickly smile on his mouth, as though he hadn't expected this kind of backfire. "Look," he said, but his voice was drowned out in the roar of the kids as they rushed forward with Jimbo. Ronnie turned and tried to run for his bunk, but Jimbo caught his collar from behind, and pulled him backward to the ground. I saw the kid raise his baseball bat and I leaped to my feet and yelled, "Stop it! Goddamn you, stop it!"

The bat hung in midair. Slowly they turned toward me.

"It's only marbles," I said.

The camp was silent.

"It's only marbles," I repeated. "Don't you see?"

And then, because I had intruded upon a fantasy and threatened to shatter it, because the entire spiraling marbles structure was suddenly in danger, they turned from Ronnie, who was lying on the ground, and they ran toward me, shouting and screaming. Jimbo, the champion, struck me on the jaw with his fist, and when I fell to the ground, the kids began kicking me and pummeling me. There was more than anger in their blows and their whispered curses. There was conviction and an overriding necessity to convince the unbeliever as well. I refused to be convinced. I felt each deliberate blow, yes, each fierce kick, but I would not be convinced because I knew, even if they didn't, that it was only marbles.

I quit Camp Marvin early the next morning. Not because of the beating. That wasn't important. I carried my two suitcases all around the lake to Camp Lydia. It was raining, and I got soaking wet. I waited at the gate while one of the girl campers ran to get Rebecca. She came walking through the rain wearing her dirty trenchcoat, walking with that peculiar sideward lope, her hair wet and clinging to her face.

"Come on, Beck," I said. "We're going home."

She looked at me for a long time, searching my face with her dark solemn eyes while the rain came down around us. I knew that word of the beating had traveled across the lake, but I didn't know whether she was looking for cuts and bruises or for something else.

"Are you all right?" she said at last.

"Yes, I'm fine," I said. "Becky, please go pack your things." And then, as she turned to go, I said, "Becky?"

She stopped in the center of the road with the rain streaming on her face and she looked at me curiously, her eyebrows raised, waiting.

"As soon as we get back," I said, "today, this afternoon, I'm going to talk to your father."

She stared at me a moment longer, her eyes very serious, and then gave a small nod, and a smile began forming on her face, not the usual fast-breaking smile, but a slow steady smile that was somehow very sad and very old, even though she was only nineteen.

"All right, Donald," she said.

That afternoon I went to see her father at his dental office on Fordham Road in the Bronx. It was still raining. When he heard who was calling, he told his receptionist he didn't want to see me, so I marched right in and stood beside his chair while he was working on a patient, and I said, "Dr. Goldblatt, you had better see me, because you're going to see a lot more of me from now on."

He didn't want to make a very big fuss because a patient was sitting in the chair with her mouth open, so he walked over to his receptionist and quietly asked her to get the police, but I just kept standing by the chair very calmly. He didn't know it, but I had been through the hysteria bit before, in spades, and this mild case didn't faze me at all. Finally, when he realized I wasn't going to leave, he again left his patient sitting in the chair, and he told his receptionist to never mind the police, and he led me to a private little office where we sat on opposite sides of a desk.

He looked at me with dark solemn eyes, almost as black as Rebecca's, and he said, "What the hell do you want from my life?"

"Dr. Goldblatt," I said, "I don't want anything from your life."

"Except my daughter," he said sourly.

"Yes, but that's not from *your* life, that's from *hers*."

"No," Dr. Goldblatt said.

"Dr. Goldblatt," I said politely, "I didn't come here to ask your permission to see her. I came here to tell you that we're getting engaged, and as soon as we graduate we're going to get married."

"No," Dr. Goldblatt said. "You're a Gentile, she's a Jewish girl, it would never work. Don't you know the trouble you're asking for? Different religions, different cultures, how will you raise the children, what will you . . . ?"

"Dr. Goldblatt," I said, "that's only marbles."

"What?"

"I said it's only marbles."

The office went very silent, just the way the camp had when I'd shouted those words the day before. Dr. Goldblatt looked at me for a long time, his face expressionless. Then, all he said was "Marbles."

"Yes," I said, "marbles. Dr. Goldblatt, I'm going to pick up Becky at the house tonight at eight o'clock. At the *house*, Dr. Goldblatt. I'm not going to meet her in some dark alley any more."

Dr. Goldblatt said nothing.

"Because she's too nice to be meeting in dark alleys," I said, "and I love her."

Dr. Goldblatt still said nothing.

"Well," I said, "it was nice talking to you."

I got up and offered my hand to him, which he refused. I shrugged and started for the door. I had my hand on the knob when I heard him say behind me, "Marbles. *This* is what my daughter picked. Marbles."

I didn't let him see me smile. I walked downstairs to the street. The rain had tapered off to a fine drizzle. The gutters ran with water, and large puddles had formed in the hollows near the curb. I could remember sticking my hand into puddles just like those long ago when I was a kid, when the loss of a hundred immies had meant a great deal to me.

I called Becky from a telephone booth in the corner drugstore.

The nut—she cried.

THE TOURISTS

THE GIANT BROWN PODS of the royal poincianas were motionless on the still hot air. Like huge, closed straight-razors, they hung lifelessly from the trees against a sky of baked blue enamel. In a few months they would bloom, but they hung in ugly limpness now in a Jamaica forsaken by the trade winds, an island aflame with tropical heat, persistent, relentless, as still as death itself.

The taxi wound its way down through the heat, the sun reflecting dizzily from its polished hood and top. The native driver honked his horn incessantly and pedestrians along the side of the road inched closer to the curb each time the horn sounded, balancing bundles on their heads, walking with the straight proud walk Michael had found absent in Nassau.

His wife sat beside him in the back of the taxi, both of them rendered mute by the intense heat. She wore a white blouse and white tapered slacks, a young blond woman, evenly tanned but still carrying on her face and in her eyes the lacquered look of the native New Yorker. The cab came down out of the hills, the bay on its right resplendently blue under the brilliant sun. Michael thought of asking the driver to stop for a moment so that he could take a picture of the curving bay. And then the moment passed, the idea seemed to require too much energy. He slouched on the back seat, squinting his eyes against the sunshine which drenched the interior of the cab, wondering why he was always forgetting his sunglasses back at the hotel. He was a tall, thin man with bright blue eyes, narrowed now in an angular face. He wore a white shirt open at the throat, and he was consciously aware of his lean good looks, imagining himself somehow as a white hunter in the heart of darkest Africa, a fantasy he knew to be absurd. And yet, not totally absurd. There *was* a primitive smell to the island and its people, a feeling that civilization was worn by the tropics as haphazardly as a badly made suit.

"I hate this town," Diane said suddenly.

He turned to look at her. Or rather, his eyes shifted toward her. He did not move his head or change his position. "It's not a bad town," he said.

"It's awful. I think we ought to go on to Haiti."

"No. I can't stand beggars."

"There are beggars, too."

"Not like Haiti," he said. "In Haiti, they're all over the streets."

"A beggar or two might be exciting."

"No, thank you. That's not my idea of a vacation."

"What *is* your idea of a vacation?" she asked. "Never mind, don't bother. I know. You want a rest."

"Exactly."

"We've been resting for two weeks. When do we take a rest from resting?"

"It's not really that dull, Diane. Actually, this is a pretty interesting town. Plenty to buy here."

"I'm not interested in the business structure of Montego Bay. And if another native urges me to buy a straw hat when any damn fool can see I'm already wearing one, I think I'll scream."

Michael laughed suddenly, a humorless laugh that rang emptily in the silent cab.

"I don't see what's so funny," she said. "I'm trying to tell you I'm bored."

"You were bored in New York, too."

"Yes, and that's why we came down here, isn't that right? For a change?"

"For a rest," he corrected.

"To get away from everyone we know—and your work, isn't that right?"

"I hate when you do that."

"Do what, for God's sake?"

"Repeat yourself."

"Oh, I don't care what you hate. We came down here to get away from all the pressures, and instead . . ."

"If there are any pressures here," Michael said, "I'd like to know about them."

"Boredom is a pressure."

"Boredom, boredom! Has it ever occurred to you that it's pretty boring to hear you *talk* about boredom all the time?"

"I'm sorry if I annoy you."

"I didn't say that."

"It sounded like that to me."

"All I said was . . . well, what I object to is the way you keep going on about the same things. Like your *life*-role, and your *search* for identity, and your *meaning* as a woman. Why don't you just relax, Diane? The trouble with women today is . . ."

"I don't want to hear your thesis on the mechanized kitchen again."

He shrugged. "All right."

"Because if you want to know the truth, you're pretty damn boring yourself."

"Me?" he asked incredulously.

"Yes, you. The Madison Avenue mastermind with his new accounts and his new slogans and his new campaigns and his sales-up-fifty-percent. I've never met anyone in my life who was so concerned with making money."

"I didn't realize," he said with cold hauteur, "that providing for one's wife and family was being overly concerned with . . ."

"There's a difference between . . ."

". . . money. I suppose I'd be better off if I were a native chopping sugar cane in the goddamn jungle and earning ten cents a week!"

"They don't chop sugar cane in the jungle."

"On the plantations then. Wherever the hell they do it. Maybe you'd enjoy that?"

"Maybe I would. It might be *real*, at least."

"Oh, here we go on the fake existence theme again. The glitter of New York, the tinsel whirl of . . ."

"Don't you ever understand anything I'm saying?" she asked angrily. "I hate it here! And, damnit, I'm catching a cold!"

"How can anyone catch a cold in the tropics?"

"I don't know how. By contact with a germ, I would imagine. I'm catching one, that's all."

"It must be psychosomatic."

"Maybe it is. Michael, for the love of God, let's move on."

"I like Jamaica," he said flatly.

"This is the Parade, sir," the driver interrupted gently. "Did you want to get out here, sir?"

"Yes, thank you, Andrews," Michael said. "We'll only be an hour or so."

"I'll wait for you in front of Issa's, sir."

"Very well," Michael said. He opened the door and stepped into the sunshine. He held his hand out to Diane and she followed him onto the curb.

"Why did you say 'Very well'?" she asked.

"What should I have said?"

"'Very well' sounds so British. You never say that in New York."

"Well, this isn't New York. This is the British West Indies."

"That's no reason for you to put on airs. The driver must be laughing himself silly."

"He isn't laughing at all. He's thinking he'll get three dollars for the ride and a two-dollar tip, that's what he's doing."

"Not *everyone* thinks the way you do, Michael," she said. "God, it's hot. Can't we get over in the shade?"

They crossed the street and began walking under the narrow awnings lining the narrow sidewalk. The natives rushed past, carrying bananas to the wharf, carrying shopping baskets, intent on their personal affairs, their clothes bright and gaudy. Bicycles flashed in the sunshine, an ancient bus creaked around the circle near the straw market, a nightime sign warned DIP YOUR LIGHTS.

"What did you mean by that?" he asked.

"By what?"

"By everyone not thinking the way I do."

"About money. Everyone doesn't think it's that import-ant. The driver may be thinking about other things."

"Like what?"

"Oh, for God's sake, Michael, like his family, or his wife, or . . . or . . . even taking a vacation in New York one day."

"He could never afford a vacation in New York."

"In Kingston then."

"He'd never be able to afford that, either."

"Well, that doesn't make him any less a man."

"What is it, Diane? Does my earning power annoy

you? Must I constantly compete with my own wife in addition to the daily . . ."

"You've told me about the Madison Avenue ratrace, thanks. Please spare me."

"I'm awfully sorry, but that's the way things are. If you think . . ."

"Then *change* the way things are! Before it's too late!"

"I'll go out and buy a machete, would that suit you? And we'll live in a lovely corrugated tin hut. And you can do wood carving while I'm out chopping sugar cane. Would that satisfy your need for self-expression?"

"It's not a joke!" she said, her voice suddenly loud on the sun-hushed street.

"All right, let's end it, Diane," he said softly.

"End what?"

"The argument." He paused, puzzled. "What did you think I meant?"

"I don't know."

They stopped stock still in the center of the street.

"The argument," he said.

"Yes. I heard you."

"Well, what did you think I meant? All I meant was the argument."

"Yes."

"Well . . ." He shrugged. "Well, let's end it, all right?"

"All right."

He nodded and tried a tentative smile. Their eyes met and held for an instant.

"Would you like a drink?" he asked.

"No. It's too early."

"Well, would you like to get out of the sun? These awnings don't help at all. I'm hot. Aren't you, Diane?"

"Yes," she said.

"Well, let's get out of the sun, all right?" He shaded his eyes and looked up the street. "There's a place." He turned to her. "Antiques. Want to give it a try?"

"If you like."

They walked up the street in silence. The building was on the opposite side of the road, its front painted a bright tropical green. The sign Michael had seen hung from a rusted wrought-iron support.

AUTHENTIC ANTIQUES
COINS   JEWELRY
BRITISH—JAMAICAN—SPANISH

An arrow pointed to a narrow flight of steps on the side of the building. The wall at the top of the steps was painted a shocking pink. The green of the building and the pink of the wall blended like the stem and bloom of a wild tropical flower, merged to give an impression of lush savagery stained with brilliant sunshine. The steps rose to the pink wall in golden fury, seemed to collide with the wall and a second painted red arrow indicating the door of the shop. They climbed the steps slowly, she moving with unconscious femininity in the form-fitting white tapered slacks, he holding her elbow and moving gracelessly beside her, his expensive camera dangling from a leather strap around his neck. As they climbed the steps, he could not resist adding, "A man has to make a living, Diane," and then they reached the landing and entered the shop and were immediately blinded.

Slowly, their eyes adjusted to the dimness of the room.

Two windows opened on the street outside and twin shafts of sunlight pierced the gloom, dust motes tirelessly climbing them to the low ceiling. The walls were hung with clocks, and clocks peered into the gloom from behind the dust-covered fronts of ancient cases. A mesh cage was at one side of the shop, enclosing a table covered with the intricate wheels and springs of a disemboweled watch, a jeweler's loupe, a miniature screwdriver, a pair of tweezers. Dust seemed to cover everything. Dust and heat permeated the shop, became the shop's lifeblood. Dust and heat seeped into every crack and corner until the shop seemed to possess a secret pulsing sound, the sound of silence and gloom and heat and dust commingled.

The old man came from behind the mesh cage, dust-colored himself, a big man wearing a white shirt and pale-blue trousers which hung sloppily over a loose paunch. A yellow silk tie was knotted carelessly about his neck. He breathed heavily as he walked toward them, his eyes touching Diane's face and then shifting slowly to Michael, who wiped sweat from his upper lip with a clean white handkerchief.

"Yes, sir?" the man said. He did not smile. His eyes were dark black in a dry face the color of dead ashes. His black hair, turning gray, clung wetly to his forehead. A laborious wheeze came from his thick lips when he spoke. "Yes, madam?"

"We're just looking," Michael said.

"For what, sir?"

"We're not sure. We ... uh ..."

Michael hesitated. He had not expected this. He had expected a neat, precise refuge from the sun, a tourist shop with a clean tourist façade and not this cluttered den of stronger heat and hanging dust.

"Some clocks, perhaps, sir? Or some coins? Or some jewelry for the lady?"

For a moment, an awkwardness crowded into the shop. Michael knew instantly that they'd made a mistake, and he could see that Diane wanted nothing more than to get out of this small dark cave. Moreover, he felt the proprietor was fully aware of their discomfort and would be happy to see them leave. But none of them wished to appear rude, and so they went through the shallow pantomime of buyer and seller, no one truly intending to buy or to sell, the awkwardness not one of intent or purpose but simply one of ineptitude, a stuttering bow to the absurd demands of civilization.

"My name is Barker," the fat man said. "This is my shop."

He extended his hand clumsily to Michael, and Michael gave it an unenthusiastic shake and then dropped it. Barker turned to Diane and extended his hand again. She took it cautiously, as if she were picking up a loathsome object preparatory to dropping it in the trash basket. Barker held her hand and brought it closer to his face as if he were about to kiss it in the Continental manner. Then, still holding it, he examined the slender fingers and said, "A ring for madam, perhaps?"

"No, I don't want a ring," Diane said briskly, pulling back her hand. "We'd better go, Michael. Our driver is waiting."

Barker smiled palely. "In Jamaica, madam," he said, "all things can wait."

"Rings included," Diane said coldly. "Let's go, Michael."

Barker stepped into their path unobtrusively, almost gliding over the dusty floor, so that his interference did not seem at all like a deliberate one, his eyes never leaving Diane.

"I have some beautiful things to show," he said. "Wait."

"I think . . ." Michael started.

"Wait," Barker said.

He went behind the counter. Michael glanced at Diane and gave a slight shrug of his shoulders. Her eyes met his coldly, more meaning in them than he could read. He frowned. Behind the counter, Barker wheezingly knelt and then came into view again, his ash-dust face appearing above the countertop, his eyes flicking again to Diane. It seemed hotter in the shop now. Barker's shirt stuck to his flaccid body, giant blots of perspiration spreading from his armpits across his chest.

"Here," he said. "Look at this, sir."

He opened the case in his hands. A dueling pistol rested on black velvet, a handsomely wrought gun with silver filigree decorating the handle and twined around the barrel.

"That is a very old gun, sir," Barker said. "Look at it, sir. It is beautiful, is it not, sir?"

"Yes, it is," Michael said honestly, leaning closer to the pistol.

"You may hold it, sir, if you like," Barker said. He handed the pistol in its case to Michael and then turned again to Diane. "That is an interesting watch you're wearing, madam," he said, and he glanced at the gold watch that hung from a chain about her throat, a small gold circle resting against the white pillow of her blouse.

"May I?" he asked, and before she could answer he reached for the watch, his thick fingers swooping toward it as gracefully and relentlessly as the vultures they had seen in Port Antonio yesterday dropping swiftly out of the sky. Delicately, his fingers plucked the watch from where it rested on her blouse. He did not touch her and yet the careful, exaggerated delicacy of his fingers as they plucked the watch from its nesting place was somehow a violation. Somehow the lack of physical contact implied a greater, more intimate, contact. He held the watch on his thick palm and glanced at Michael who was examining the silver-filigreed pistol.

"This is an old watch, madam?" he asked Diane.

"No. It's new."

"Oh, but not so new, madam."

"I bought it a year ago."

"It has the appearance of an old watch, madam."

"It's not."

"That is a shame, madam," Barker said. "For the old things have greater value."

"Only to collectors of antiques," Diane said frostily, and Michael looked up from the pistol in his hands, startled by the unusual sound of his wife's voice.

"How much is this worth?" he asked Barker.

Gently Barker allowed the pendant watch to return to its resting place. He turned wheezily to Michael, sighed, and said, "The pistol costs two hundred pounds, sir."

"It's beautiful," Michael said.

A thin smile crossed Barker's face. "But more than you care to spend, sir?"

"Oh, I wasn't considering buying it," Michael answered. "I was just curious." He wiped his lip again, and handed the pistol case back to Barker. "Come on, Diane. We'd better go."

"Wait," Barker said, and he held up a finger and looked again at Diane, and this time Michael saw the quick motion of his eyes and thought, *Why, the old man is flirting with my wife!* The thought was somewhat amusing and also somewhat irritating, a curious mixture that somehow strengthened Michael's desire to leave the shop at once.

"We really must go," he said.

"Just one moment, sir," Barker said. "I have something else to show you."

Michael turned to Diane. She rested against the dusty counter leaning on one elbow, the pendant watch hanging, a negative silhouette in gleaming white, a graceful curving silhouette from the tilt of her blond head to the long lissome length of her legs in the tight tapered slacks. An odd smile was on her mouth, a smile Michael had never seen there before. She did not move from the counter. She kept staring at the old man as he went to one of the ancient cases and pulled open a heavy drawer and then moved toward them with a large carved wooden chest in his hands.

"Let's go, Diane," Michael said. She seemed not to hear him. "Diane," he said. "Let's go."

"No," she answered. "Let's see this."

Their eyes met for an instant, and he thought frozenly, *She's enjoying the old man's attention,* but he knew this was ridiculous—and yet there was the smile on his wife's face. He wiped again at his lip with his handkerchief. In the street outside, he could hear the rushed babble of native speech and honking horns and sandaled feet beating the scorched pavement. Barker approached, and the ticking of all the clocks in the shop suddenly registered on Michael's ears, a sound that had surely been there all along but which he heard only now, the ticking of hundreds of clocks, and yet a ticking that was timeless, a ticking that was somehow not at all connected with the passage of time but that seemed instead to nullify it and render it meaningless.

"Let's go," he said sharply, but Barker was standing in their path again, his obese body wedged into the small entrance area between the counters. He held out the wooden chest, smiled wanly at Diane, and said, "Would madam care to open it?'

"Thank you," Diane said, and this time there was an unmistakable lilt to her voice, and she arched one eyebrow coquettishly. She smiled at the old man, a lazy, mysterious smile, and then she slowly lifted the lid of the chest.

The beam of sunlight from the open window caught the contents of the box, magnified the hundreds of thick gold coins which were heaped inside. The sight of the coins was startling to Michael. He had held no preconceived notion of what the chest contained and now that it was opened, splashed with sunlight, each coin glittering with a thick circular life of its own, he caught his breath in wonder and surprise and unconsciously moved closer to the heavy chest as Barker set it down on the countertop.

"Doubloons," Barker said. "Spanish doubloons. They are worth a fortune, sir." His eyes met Diane's over the open chest. There was a fine sheen of sweat on Diane's forehead and her upper lip. The old man's mouth was twitching slightly. His hand on the open lid of the chest had begun to tremble.

"Would you like to examine one, sir?" he asked, but he did not deliver the words to Michael. He spoke to Diane, and his eyes held hers in a steady gaze now, and she smiled back at him in a frozen, sleepy-eyed way, her eyes meeting the old man's over the open box like a challenge. Michael picked up one of the coins. It was heavy and thick, inscribed with Spanish lettering and the name of a monarch and a seventeenth-century date. The chest was full of them. He wanted suddenly to pick them up and let them trickle through his open fingers.

"Would you like that coin, sir?" Barker said. There was a tremor in the old man's voice now.

"It's very beautiful," Michael whispered.

"It is very very beautiful, sir. Would you like it, sir?"

"How . . . how much is it?"

"There is a price, sir."

"What's the price?"

"What do you think the coin is worth, sir?"

"I have no idea."

"It is worth a great deal, sir."

"Well, how much?"

"Make me an offer, sir."

"I told you," Michael said, annoyed, "I don't know how much it's worth." He had become irritated suddenly and irrationally, irritated by the old man's trembling hand and by the frozen smile on Diane's face, and by the dust and suffocating heat of the shop, and the rush of noise outside, and irritated too by the sight of the gleaming coins in the old wooden chest.

"I will accept a reasonable offer, sir," Barker persisted.

"I told you I . . ."

"For two coins then, sir? Would you make an offer for two of the coins?"

"If I don't know what one is worth, how can I . . ."

"Three, sir? Will you barter for three?"

He looked into the old man's eyes, and he saw what was there, and the old man's meaning cracked sharply into his mind, and he felt a sudden chill.

"A dozen coins, sir?" Barker said, and he leaned closer, and his eyes turned to Diane, coveted her in one swift glance, and somehow assured her, assured her of something certain that was about to happen, and Michael realized with a shock that he wanted those coins, he desired those coins in the wooden chest, he wanted them desperately, and it was then that his eyes narrowed and the dust in the shop took on a new and different smell.

"Two dozen coins, sir? I am willing to trade. I am willing to barter."

Michael held the single doubloon in his hand and he looked at the glittering heap of coins and felt suddenly weak. He began shaking his head, the ticking of the clocks loud in his ears, the dust motes recklessly climbing the golden shafts, Diane blond and smiling her cold fixed evil smile, the old man leaning forward and wheezing heavily, anxiously awaiting his answer, evil, and the stench of evil in his own nostrils, suffocating him. He reached for Diane's arm blindly, and he dropped the doubloon onto the gleaming pile of coins and shoved past the old man. Barker reached out as if to stop them, and his thick fingers traveled the length of Diane's naked arm caressingly as she rushed past, recoiling from his touch, and went swiftly down the steps into the street, Michael following behind her, the expensive camera swinging from his neck.

They stopped on the sidewalk. The sun was still intense. Behind them the steps rose to the ugly pink wall and the beckoning red arrow. His hand shook as he fumbled for the cigarettes in the pocket of his white shirt.

"He recognized us," Diane whispered, and suddenly she began to shiver.

"Yes," Michael answered quickly, taking her elbow. His eyes would not meet hers. "He knew we were tourists."

ON THE SIDEWALK, BLEEDING

THE BOY LAY bleeding in the rain. He was sixteen years old, and he wore a bright purple silk jacket, and the lettering across the back of the jacket read THE ROYALS. The boy's name was Andy, and the name was delicately scripted in black thread on the front of the jacket, just over the heart. *Andy.*

He had been stabbed ten minutes ago. The knife had entered just below his rib cage and had been drawn across his body violently, tearing a wide gap in his flesh. He lay on the sidewalk with the March rain drilling his jacket and drilling his body and washing away the blood that poured from his open wound. He had known excruciating pain when the knife had torn across his body, and then sudden comparative relief when the blade was pulled away. He had heard the voice saying, "That's for you, Royal!" and then the sound of footsteps hurrying into the rain, and then he had fallen to the sidewalk, clutching his stomach, trying to stop the flow of blood.

He tried to yell for help, but he had no voice. He did not know why his voice had deserted him, or why the rain had suddenly become so fierce, or why there was an open hole in his body from which his life ran redly, steadily. It was 11.30 P.M., but he did not know the time.

There was another thing he did not know.

He did not know he was dying. He lay on the sidewalk, bleeding, and he thought only: *That was a fierce rumble. They got me good that time,* but he did not know he was dying. He would have been frightened had he known. In his ignorance, he lay bleeding and wishing he could cry out for help, but there was no voice in his throat. There was only the bubbling of blood between his lips whenever he opened his mouth to speak. He lay silent in his pain, waiting, waiting for someone to find him.

He could hear the sound of automobile tires hushed on the muzzle of rainswept streets, far away at the other end of the long alley. He lay with his face pressed to the sidewalk, and he could see the splash of neon far away at the other end of the alley, tinting the pavement red and green, slickly brilliant in the rain.

He wondered if Laura would be angry.

He had left the jump to get a package of cigarettes. He had told her he would be back in a few minutes, and then he had gone downstairs and found the candy store closed. He knew that Alfredo's on the next block would be open until at least two, and he had started through the alley, and that was when he'd been ambushed. He could hear the faint sound of music now, coming from a long, long way off, and he wondered if Laura was dancing, wondered if she had missed him yet. Maybe she thought he wasn't coming back. Maybe she thought he'd cut out for good. Maybe she'd already left the jump and gone home. He thought of her face, the brown eyes and the jet-black hair, and thinking of her he forgot his pain a little, forgot that blood was rushing from his body. Someday he would marry Laura. Someday he would marry her, and they would have a lot of kids, and then they would get out of the neighborhood. They would move to a clean project in the Bronx, or maybe they would move to Staten Island. When they were married, when they had kids. . . .

He heard footsteps at the other end of the alley, and he lifted his cheek from the sidewalk and looked into the darkness and tried to cry out, but again there was only a soft hissing bubble of blood on his mouth.

The man came down the alley. He had not seen Andy yet. He walked, and then stopped to lean against the brick of the building, and then walked again. He saw Andy then and came toward him, and he stood over him for a long time, the minutes ticking, ticking, watching him and not speaking.

Then he said, "What's a matter, buddy?"

Andy could not speak, and he could barely move. He lifted his face slightly and looked up at the man, and in the rainswept alley he smelled the sickening odor of alcohol and realized the man was drunk. He did not feel any particular panic. He did not know he was dying, and so he felt only mild disappointment that the man who had found him was drunk.

The man was smiling.

"Did you fall down, buddy?" he asked. "You mus' be as drunk as I am." He grinned, seemed to remember why he had entered the alley in the first place, and said, "Don' go way. I'll be ri' back."

The man lurched away. Andy heard his footsteps, and then the sound of the man colliding with a garbage can, and some mild swearing, and then the sound of the man urinating, lost in the steady wash of the rain. He waited for the man to come back.

It was 11.39.

When the man returned, he squatted alongside Andy. He studied him with drunken dignity.

"You gonna catch cold here," he said. "What's a matter? You like layin' in the wet?"

Andy could not answer. The man tried to focus his eyes on Andy's face. The rain spattered around them.

"You like a drink?"

Andy shook his head.

"I gotta bottle. Here," the man said. He pulled a pint bottle from his inside jacket pocket. He uncapped it and extended it to Andy. Andy tried to move, but pain wrenched him back flat against the sidewalk.

"Take it," the man said. He kept watching Andy. "Take it." When Andy did not move, he said, "Nev' mind, I'll have one m'self." He tilted the bottle to his lips, and then wiped the back of his hand across his mouth. "You too young to be drinkin', anyway. Should be 'shamed of yourself, drunk an' layin' in a alley, all wet. Shame on you. I gotta good minda calla cop."

Andy nodded. Yes, he tried to say. Yes, call a cop. Please. Call one.

"Oh, you don' like that, huh?" the drunk said. "You don' wanna cop to fin' you all drunk an' wet in a alley, huh? Okay, buddy. This time you get off easy." He got to his feet. "This time you lucky," he said. He waved broadly at Andy, and then almost lost his footing. "S'long, buddy," he said.

Wait, Andy thought. *Wait, please, I'm bleeding.*

"S'long," the drunk said again. "I see you aroun'," and then he staggered off up the alley.

Andy lay and thought: *Laura, Laura. Are you dancing?*

The couple came into the alley suddenly. They ran into the alley together, running from the rain, the boy holding the girl's elbow, the girl spreading a newspaper over her head to protect her hair. Andy lay crumpled against the pavement, and he watched them run into the alley laughing, and then duck into the doorway not ten feet from him.

"Man, what rain!" the boy said. "You could drown out there."

"I have to get home," the girl said. "It's late, Freddie. I have to get home."

"We got time," Freddie said. "Your people won't raise a fuss if you're a little late. Not with this kind of weather."

"It's dark," the girl said, and she giggled.

"Yeah," the boy answered, his voice very low.

"Freddie . . . ?"

"Um?"

"You're . . . you're standing very close to me."

"Um."

There was a long silence. Then the girl said, "Oh," only that single word, and Andy knew she'd been kissed, and he suddenly hungered for Laura's mouth. It was then that he wondered if he would ever kiss Laura again. It was then that he wondered if he was dying.

No, he thought, *I can't be dying, not from a little street rumble, not from just getting cut. Guys get cut all the time in rumbles. I can't be dying. No, that's stupid. That don't make any sense at all.*

"You shouldn't," the girl said.

"Why not?"

"I don't know."

"Do you like it?"

"Yes."

"So?"

"I don't know."

"I love you, Angela," the boy said.

"I love you, too, Freddie," the girl said, and Andy listened and thought: *I love you, Laura. Laura, I think maybe I'm dying. Laura, this is stupid but I think maybe I'm dying. Laura, I think I'm dying!*

He tried to speak. He tried to move. He tried to crawl toward the doorway where he could see the two figures in embrace. He tried to make a noise, a sound, and a grunt came from his lips, and then he tried again, and another grunt came, a low animal grunt of pain.

"What was that?" the girl said, suddenly alarmed, breaking away from the boy.

"I don't know," he answered.

"Go look, Freddie."

"No. Wait."

Andy moved his lips again. Again the sound came from him.

"Freddie!"

"What?"

"I'm scared."

"I'll go see," the boy said.

He stepped into the alley. He walked over to where Andy lay on the ground. He stood over him, watching him.

"You all right?" he asked.

"What is it?" Angela said from the doorway.

"Somebody's hurt," Freddie said.

"Let's get out of here," Angela said.

"No. Wait a minute." He knelt down beside Andy. "You cut?" he asked.

Andy nodded. The boy kept looking at him. He saw the lettering on the jacket then. THE ROYALS. He turned to Angela.

"He's a Royal," he said.

"Let's . . . what . . . what do you want to do, Freddie?"

"I don't know. I don't want to get mixed up in this. He's a Royal. We help him, and the Guardians'll be down on our necks. I don't want to get mixed up in this, Angela."

"Is he . . . is he hurt bad?"

"Yeah, it looks that way."

"What shall we do?"

"I don't know."

"We can't leave him here in the rain." Angela hesitated. "Can we?"

"If we get a cop, the Guardians'll find out who," Freddie said. "I don't know, Angela. I don't know."

Angela hesitated a long time before answering. Then she said, "I have to get home, Freddie. My people will begin to worry."

"Yeah," Freddie said. He looked at Andy again. "You all right?" he asked. Andy lifted his face from the sidewalk, and his eyes said: *Please, please help me,* and maybe Freddie read what his eyes were saying, and maybe he didn't.

Behind him, Angela said, "Freddie, let's get out of here! Please!" There was urgency in her voice, urgency bordering on the edge of panic. Freddie stood up. He looked at Andy again, and then mumbled. "I'm sorry," and then he took Angela's arm and together they ran toward the neon splash at the other end of the alley.

Why, they're afraid of the Guardians, Andy thought in amazement. *But why should they be? I wasn't afraid of the Guardians. I never turkeyed out of a rumble with the Guardians. I got heart. But I'm bleeding.*

The rain was soothing somehow. It was a cold rain, but his body was hot all over, and the rain helped to cool him. He had always liked rain. He could remember sitting in Laura's house one time, the rain running down the windows, and just looking out over the street, watching the people running from the rain. That was when he'd first joined the Royals. He could remember how happy he was the Royals had taken him. The Royals and the Guardians, two of the biggest. He was a Royal. There had been meaning to the title.

Now, in the alley, with the cold rain washing his hot body, he wondered about the meaning. If he died, he was Andy. He was not a Royal. He was simply Andy, and he was dead. And he wondered suddenly if the Guardians who had ambushed him and knifed him had ever once realized he was Andy? Had they known that he was Andy, or had they simply known that he was a Royal wearing a purple silk jacket? Had they stabbed *him*, Andy, or had they only stabbed the jacket and the title, and what good was the title if you were dying?

I'm Andy, he screamed wordlessly. *For Christ's sake, I'm Andy!*

An old lady stopped at the other end of the alley. The garbage cans were stacked there, beating noisily in the rain. The old lady carried an umbrella with broken ribs, carried it with all the dignity of a queen. She stepped into the mouth of the alley, a shopping bag over one arm. She lifted the lids of the garbage cans delicately, and she did not hear Andy grunt because she was a little deaf and because the rain was beating a steady relentless tattoo on the cans. She had been searching and foraging for the better part of the night. She collected her string and her newspapers, and an old hat with a feather on it from one of the garbage cans, and a broken footstool from another of the cans. And then she delicately replaced the lids and lifted her umbrella high and walked out of the alley mouth with queenly dignity. She had worked swiftly and soundlessly, and now she was gone.

The alley looked very long now. He could see people passing at the other end of it, and he wondered who the people were, and he wondered if he would ever get to know them, wondered who it was on the Guardians who had stabbed him, who had plunged the knife into his body.

"That's for you, Royal!" the voice had said, and then the footsteps, his arms being released by the others, the fall to the pavement. "That's for you, Royal!" Even in his pain, even as he collapsed, there had been some sort of pride in knowing he was a Royal. Now there was no pride at all. With the rain beginning to chill him, with the blood pouring steadily between his fingers, he knew only a sort of dizziness, and within the giddy dizziness, he could only think: *I want to be Andy.*

It was not very much to ask of the world.

He watched the world passing at the other end of the alley. The world didn't know he was Andy. The world didn't know he was alive. He wanted to say, "Hey, I'm alive! Hey, look at me! I'm alive! Don't you know I'm alive? Don't you know I exist?"

He felt weak and very tired. He felt alone and wet and feverish and chilled, and he knew he was going to die now, and the knowledge made him suddenly sad. He was not frightened. For some reason, he was not frightened. He was only filled with an overwhelming sadness that his life would be over at sixteen. He felt all at once as if he had never done anything, never seen anything, never been anywhere. There were so many things to do, and he wondered why he'd never thought of them before, wondered why the rumbles and the jumps and the purple jacket had always seemed so important to him before, and now they seemed like such small things in a world he was missing, a world that was rushing past at the other end of the alley.

I don't want to die, he thought. *I haven't lived yet.*

It seemed very important to him that he take off the purple jacket. He was very close to dying, and when they found him, he did not want them to say, "Oh, it's a Royal." With great effort, he rolled over onto his back. He felt the pain tearing at his stomach when he moved, a pain he did not think was possible. But he wanted to take off the jacket. If he never did another thing, he wanted to take off the jacket. The jacket had only one meaning now, and that was a very simple meaning.

If he had not been wearing the jacket, he would not have been stabbed. The knife had not been plunged in hatred of Andy. The knife hated only the purple jacket. The jacket was a stupid meaningless thing that was robbing him of his life. He wanted the jacket off his back. With an enormous loathing, he wanted the jacket off his back.

He lay struggling with the shiny wet material. His arms were heavy, and pain ripped fire across his body whenever he moved. But he squirmed and fought and twisted until one arm was free and then the other, and then he rolled away from the jacket and lay quite still, breathing heavily, listening to the sound of his breathing and the sound of the rain and thinking: *Rain is sweet, I'm Andy.*

She found him in the alleyway a minute past midnight. She left the dance to look for him, and when she found him she knelt beside him and said, "Andy, it's me, Laura."

He did not answer her. She backed away from him, tears springing into her eyes, and then she ran from the alley hysterically and did not stop running until she found the cop.

And now, standing with the cop, she looked down at him, and the cop rose and said, "He's dead," and all the crying was out of her now. She stood in the rain and said nothing, looking at the dead boy on the pavement, and looking at the purple jacket that rested a foot away from his body.

The cop picked up the jacket and turned it over in his hands.

"A Royal, huh?" he said.

The rain seemed to beat more steadily now, more fiercely.

She looked at the cop and, very quietly, she said, "His name is Andy."

The cop slung the jacket over his arm. He took out his black pad, and he flipped it open to a blank page.

"A Royal," he said.

Then he began writing.

IT WAS LOVELY THAT SUMMER

HE COULD SEE the Black Knight through the slitted metal strips of his face visor. He had drawn up alongside the small bridge running over the stream, his armor glinting in the sunshine, his shield flashing with wrought silver falcons that streaked across the black as if in living flight.

He felt no fear.

He faced the knight, and he could feel the solid flanks of his stallion beneath him, could feel the weight of his own armor, could hear the myriad splintering sounds of the forest everywhere around him, the birds and insects hurling epithets to the skies. And then suddenly the woods were still, as if every living creature had heard the terrifying muting sound of approaching menace. The horses sniffed fitfully at the silent air and then simultaneously broke into a trot across the wide tufted clearing. He held his lance in his right hand, balanced loosely there, the flaring fluted butt jogging against his hip as the horse gathered speed and then rode into a clod-loosening gallop. The Black Knight filled the sky, loomed immensely against the yellow sunlight, his tilting helm pointed like the prow of a ship, cleaving the air with . . .

"Barry! Barry!"

. . . a swishing sound that penetrated to his own helmet and the leather padding beneath. He could feel the sudden sweat on his hands under their protective mail. In a moment, lance would . . .

"Barry, where are you? Are you upstairs?"

. . . splinter against lance, horses would buck and rear in lathering armor-plated . . .

"Barry, won't you please answer me?"

He heard the voice, and he came up slowly, slowly, like a man swimming through a dense sea of yellow molasses. The hoofbeats still pounded in his ears, the armor of the enemy knight glittered for an instant longer and then vanished completely. He found himself staring at the rows of letters on his typewriter, and then he sighed deeply.

"Yes, dear," he said. "I'm upstairs."

He could hear her heavy tread on the steps leading to the attic. She stopped in the doorway and, for an instant in the deepening dusk, he visualized her as she once had been. She smiled gently and came into the room, shattering the image like the broken surface of a secret pool.

"What are you doing, Barry?" she asked.

"I . . . I was trying to write a story," he said.

"Again?"

"Yes."

He was not a good-looking man, and had never been one. At forty-seven, his sandy hair was beginning to thin, and he had acquired the stoop-shouldered stance that came to many accountants after years of bending over books. He was not thin, but there was a gauntness about his faded blue eyes which made him seem far older than he actually was. He reached for the sheet of paper in the machine now, pulled it slowly and carefully from the roller, and laid it beside the typewriter.

"What kind of a story?" his wife asked. He had never known her to raise her voice in all the years they'd been married, but there was a peculiar gentleness to her words now, as if she knew she was intruding on a private glade and as a result walked softly and delicately.

"A story about knights," he said, raising his eyes quickly to meet hers, afraid she would laugh, relieved when she did not.

"Like the ones we saw in the castle that summer?" she asked.

"The castle?"

"Don't you remember the armor?" she said. "In the castle? The summer we spent in England?" She paused. "The summer we were married, Barry."

"Yes," he said. "Of course."

"It must be fun to be able to put one's thoughts on paper."

"Well, I'm pretty new at it," Barry said.

"Still, I wish I could write stories." A fleeting smile touched her mouth. "Stories about knights and their ladies." The smile vanished on a sigh. "Did you forget the Fullers were coming tonight?"

"The Fullers? I'm sorry. I'd forgotten."

"That's all right. You still have time to change your shirt and put on a tie." She looked at the typewriter. "Knights," she said softly. "What fun."

They started down the attic steps. He walked several paces behind her, watching her as he would a stranger, noticing the thick ankles and the heavily padded waist and wondering where the girl Ellen Frazer had gone, realizing that she had disappeared almost the instant she became Mrs. Barry Randolph. And then denying the realization, knowing that time was more subtle than that, knowing that time had only slowly robbed him of the lovely slender girl he had known, and replaced her with someone he still loved and yet, and yet . . .

He felt so sad, all at once.

Following his wife down the attic steps, he thought how much he'd enjoyed the story he was writing.

He got out of bed at two o'clock that morning, long after the Fullers had gone home.

Ellen was asleep in the twin bed beside him, her mouth open, the faint snore filling the silent bedroom. He had never told her that she sometimes snored. He knew she would have been embarrassed, and he could not have faced her embarrassment. And so he had kept the knowledge secret, annoyed by it and feeling oddly guilty, as if he were keeping something of great importance from the woman he loved. Still, he knew he would never tell her.

He put on a robe, tiptoed out of the room, and went upstairs to the attic. He turned on the small light over his work table, took a sheet of typing paper from the box, inserted it into the machine, and began typing. There was a smile on his face as he worked. He got into the feel of the story easily, more easily each time as a matter of fact. The room around him began to dissolve almost instantly, and another world swarmed into his mind, a world of bannerettes and pennoncels, of ladies in long pointed caps with gossamer veils floating behind on the fair wind— and there, there high on the hill against a periwinkle sky, the battlements of the castle where they sat, and the mocking bird twittering in the open courtyard below.

The lady Ellen had never looked lovelier.

She sat with her embroidery in her lap, and she asked, "And why did you smite him so, Barry? It is said his helmet came unlaced and that his shield was rent in two."

"All of which he deserved, and more."

The lady Ellen giggled and held her hand to her mouth. "But why?"

"He has of late been saying things," Barry said.

"Oh?" Her green eyes twinkled for an instant, flashed with the sudden unexpected glow of emerald. Her hair was blonde, and it trailed past a slender neck, fell over the curve of breasts which richly threatened the low neck of her bodice. Slender ankles showed delicately at the hem of her long blue skirt. Her hands, ever busy, threaded the needle back and forth through the hoop. A ruby in a golden band glistened on her right forefinger. "And what things has he been saying?"

"He has spoken ill of thee," he said, using the knightly language, accompanying his words with a slight tilt of his head, feeling strangely awkward, and yet supremely confident. "Of thee, fair Ellen."

"Barry!"

The lady Ellen blushed. He had not thought such beauty possible. The blush started at the base of her throat, flowered in pink abandon, spread to her cheekbones and then seemed to touch the emerald eyes with a deeper glow. She lowered her head and he saw her face in profile against a placid sky, and he longed to cup her cheeks with his hands and . . .

"Barry, is that you? Barry?"

. . . kiss the mouth, the petal buds of that incredible mouth, hold her in his arms and tell her of his love, hold her against the pounding of his heart . . .

"Barry?"

. . . beneath the silken tunic and tell her of the things he knew, the things he felt, the things that . . .

. . . that ached inside . . .

. . . that . . . that longed inside to . . .

. . . to . . . to . . .

He blinked.

The image was fading. The girl in the long blue gown reached out for him, as if unwilling to let him go, one delicate hand extended, the gold thimble flashing on her finger, reaching, reaching, her mouth rounding in short and instant pain, the sunlight fading behind her, the blue sky melting, melting, the blonde hair gone, the eyes pleading, entreating, *Barry, Barry, take me with you,* and then fading, fading, and she was gone.

"What?" he said. "What?"

It had taken a long time this time, a long time for the image to fade, a long time for him to break away from the typewritten page and return to the attic room. He could not imagine how long. He knew only that his wife was silent downstairs, and he suspected that she had fallen asleep again. Wearily, he turned out the light and went down to the bedroom. She was sitting up in bed, her hair in pincurls, hair that had once been as blonde as sunwash, now streaked with gray, no longer resilient with the tautness of youth. She did not turn when he came into the room. She sat quite still, looking at the wall.

"Ellen?" he said.

She did not turn.

"Ellen?"

And still she did not seem to hear him.

"*Ellen!*" he said sharply.

She turned and stared at him unrecognizingly. And then her eyes seemed to come into focus. She shook her head and said, "Oh, forgive me, Barry. I must have fallen asleep."

"No," he said. "Your eyes were open."

"What time is it, anyway? It seems so very ..." She paused. "Didn't I ... didn't I hear you typing upstairs, Barry?" A puzzled look came into her eyes. "Yes, of course. That was what woke me, the typing. And I called to you. Several times. I'm sure I called to you."

"Yes, you did."

"But then . . ." She frowned. "I *must* have fallen asleep, Barry. People don't dream unless they're asleep, do they?"

"Were you dreaming, Ellen?"

"Oh, yes, yes, a lovely dream. We were young, Barry. So very, very young. And . . . and on our honeymoon again. In England. Do you remember our honeymoon?"

"Yes, of course I do." He pulled back the blanket and got into bed.

"But if was different somehow. In the dream, I mean. In the dream . . . it . . . it was an older England. We . . . we seemed to be in medieval dress, Barry."

"Mmmm?"

"Yes, as if . . . as if you were a knight and I was a . . . a lady." She smiled in embarrassment. "Well, dreams are always silly. But it was pleasant, and it did remind me of our honeymoon." She paused reflectively. "It was lovely in England that summer. When we were young."

"Mmmm."

"It was lovely that summer," she said.

"Mmmm," he answered, and he turned out the light.

On his lunch hour the next day, he ate quickly, and then went to the receptionist's desk in the corridor. He sat at her typewriter, inserted a sheet of paper into the roller, and began typing at once, amazed at how fast the words came to him. It was as if everything were waiting behind this huge thick wooden door to which he alone had the key. He would insert the key into a keyhole framed with ornate wrought iron, and the door would swing back on massive hinges, and he would stride into a valley green with summer. And in this summer valley, the sky was always blue and the sunlight was golden and the clouds were a startling white. The people were young. The people were young, and they talked in gentle voices. The young men stood tall, and the young women were beautiful beyond imagination.

And the most beautiful of all was the lady Ellen.

"And he has said in public," she told him, "before the knights assembled, that you will be dead before the week has done. He has said that he will kill you with no mercy."

"Nor have I asked for any," Barry answered.

"Aye, and this full well he knows." She paused. "And knows he too there is no quarrel here but which is thinly founded."

"Then why does he wish me dead?"

"For two reasons, Barry."

"And they are?"

"He wishes first to revenge your meeting by the bridge where, for all the world to see, you did cover his shining black armor with dust as thick as his own shame."

"And for such knightly sport does he wish me dead?"

"Aye, for this, and for another reason," the lady Ellen said.

"Which is?"

"Which is that I love thee, Barry," she said.

"And I thee," he answered simply.

"Yes. And so must we flee. Before he kills you."

"I flee no man," Barry said.

"You flee not a man but an *army*," she answered. "He will not come alone."

"Then I will seek him out alone, and slay him first."

"And afterward?" she asked. "Afterward when they have found him dead and know whereat to lay the deed?"

"Then . . . then . . ."

"Then will you flee?"

"Where?"

"To another valley," she said.

"Perhaps."

"And will you take me with you?" She rushed into his arms, and she said, "Barry, Barry," and the words came to him like a murmur on the wind, a murmur carried from another valley beyond the hills, and then he felt her lips against his throat, and she whispered, *Take me with you, Barry. Take me with you!*

"I must first . . ."

"Barry, take me with you. When you have slain him, come for me. Come for me. Come for me."

He squeezed his eyes shut tightly. "Ellen . . ."

"Getting to be quite a typist, ain't you, Mr. Randolph?" the voice said.

"Ellen, when I have slain him . . ."

"You wouldn't be bucking for my job, would you, Mr. Randolph?"

He looked up from the keyboard sharply. The receptionist was standing by the desk, an ugly grin on her carefully lipsticked and rouged face.

"Ellen," he whispered urgently. "I will! I will!"

But the image was gone, and the receptionist only said, "Huh?"

The typewriter was going in the attic.

Sitting up in bed, she could hear the machine going furiously. The rattling of the keys echoed through the entire house. The bonging of the carriage bell seemed to shake the walls.

She thought she heard him call her name, and she sat up

suddenly in bed, and still the word "Ellen!" echoed through the house above the noise of the typewriter.

"Barry?" she called.

He did not answer her. The typing persisted at a maniacal pace, almost inhuman, frenzied and mechanical.

"Barry, are you all right?" she asked, suddenly alarmed.

And again she thought she heard the single word "Ellen!"

She swung her legs over the side of the bed, put on a robe, and started up toward the attic. She was halfway up the long flight of steps when the typing stopped. It stopped suddenly, and it did not begin again. She felt a sudden breeze on the stairway, as if something had passed her rapidly, a chill that forced her to pull her robe more tightly closed. She went to the top of the flight and stood in the doorway.

The attic room was empty.

A single light was burning over the work table in the center of the room. The typewriter was on the table under the light. A sheet of paper was in the carriage.

"Barry?" she said, but there was no answer. "Barry?"

For a moment, she did not want to enter the room. For a moment, she felt oddly frightened. She hesitated, her brow furrowed, and then she pulled back her shoulders and went into the attic, directly to the typewriter.

"Barry?"

There was no answer.

"Wh . . . where are you?"

Her voice echoed back at her. Her eye fell again on the sheet of paper in the machine. She reached for it and pulled it from the roller. And she read:

The black Knight was dead.

He rode across the valley now with summer in his heart toward the castle on the hill where she waited for him. The sky was blue and the bannerettes were laced with golden sunshine, and the pounding of his horse's hooves echoed the sound of youth in his heart, echoed the single word that shouted there, Ellen, Ellen, Ellen, Ellen . . .

"Barry!" she screamed. "Barry!"

And she hugged the sheet of paper to her breast with sudden ferocity, and she stared at the shadows in the attic room, a woman whose waist was thick and whose ankles were no longer slender, a woman whose blonde hair was threaded with coarser white, and the tears sprang to eyes that had once been as green as emerald, and in a keening voice, she said, "Why didn't you take me with you? Why didn't you take me with you?"

HUMAN SHARKS

IT ALL STARTED when the four of us got picked up for being out of uniform in Nagasaki. This sounds terrible, and it can mean anything from running down the street without your trousers on to climbing a Buddha bare-chested.

Actually, we had our cuffs rolled up and our white caps on the back of our heads. Out of uniform.

Frank Bishop tried to explain this to the SP, but the guy was a thick-headed ox who kept repeating, "I only know what my superiors tell me." So he hauled us into his jeep and then took us to a lieutenant jg with a Southern accent and thick, horn-rimmed glasses. The jg wiped off his sweating lenses, took our liberty cards, and promptly sent us back to the ship.

Frank kept complaining all the way out.

"Out of uniform," he said. "What are you supposed to do on a hot day? Suffocate?"

Mike Grody shrugged. "So we lose a liberty. So what?"

Mike was a thin boy, with unruly curly hair. Alongside Frank, who weighed two hundred pounds in sneakers and bath towel, he looked something like a slightly-used pipe cleaner.

"The old man ain't gonna like this," Jack O'Doole said. He had a cherubic face framed with dark black hair. His mother, he'd told us, still spoke with an Irish brogue, and couldn't taste food because she couldn't smell. I still couldn't figure what one thing had to do with the other, but I guess Jack knew his own mother better than I did.

I didn't say anything about the whole damned mess. I

was thinking of a small, sloe-eyed gal I called Tinki San. I was thinking of her and cursing the SP upside down and backwards when *Bessie* loomed up out of the mist and the launch pulled alongside her. *Bessie* is really the U.S.S. *Bessemer*, DD 142, one of the finest destroyers afloat. *Bessie*, as they said in the writeups we got after the Iwo Jima invasion, was "a term of affection used by the crew."

We climbed the ladder to the quarterdeck, saluted the colors, and then reported to Mr. Abrahams, who was Officer of the Deck.

"Back so soon?" he asked.

"Some lousy SP picked us up," Frank said.

"Oh? What for?"

"Out of uniform," Mike said blankly.

"Oh." Mr. Abrahams just nodded. I knew he was thinking of what the old man would do about our alleged misconduct. "Well," he said at length, "guess I'd better inform the captain."

I thought of Tinki San again, and then a sour taste came gushing up into my mouth as I thought of the captain.

He reacted just the way we knew he would. He gave us what is affectionately called a Captain's Mast by the crew. This is really a trial without jury, the old man being the judge. We stood at attention in our dress blues while Chief Petty Officer Calucci read off the charges.

The old man's blue eyes narrowed, and his lips clamped together.

"Out of uniform, Captain Daniels," the Chief said. "Picked up about four blocks from the base."

"Out of uniform, eh?" the old man asked.

"Yes sir," the Chief repeated tiredly.

"What do you have to say for yourselves?" the old man asked.

"Our cuffs were just rolled . . ." Frank started to answer.

Captain Daniels cut him short with a wave of his hand. "Your cuffs carry the insignia of your rate," he said. "You should exhibit your rate proudly, whether you're an apprentice seaman or a petty officer. And you should wear your uniforms proudly."

"Yes, sir," Frank said.

"I want you men to remember this," the captain continued. "When you're ashore, you are not only representatives of *my* ship, you are also representatives of the United States Navy. And in this capacity, you are ambassadors of the United States of America. The United States and I will not stand for sloppy ambassadors."

He paused and cleared his throat, and I wondered how many times he'd walked around with his cuffs rolled up on a hot day. Hell, he was a full Commander. His silver oak leaves twinkled in the sun as he prepared to speak again.

"This will be just a warning, gentlemen."

My heart jumped up into my throat at his words. *Just a warning.* Maybe the old man had a heart after all. Maybe all that talk about his coronary equipment consisting of a .45 slug was just scuttlebutt.

"I'm asking Chief Calucci to mark this on your records. If you're ever picked up on the same charge again, it'll be piss and punk for you."

Frank had already begun to smile. This was going to be a snap. I was feeling pretty good, too.

"For now, we will restrict you to the ship for two weeks."

I saw Frank's mouth drop open, and Mike turned a few shades whiter.

"Two . . . weeks?" Jack asked. "Without liberty, sir?"

"If you can't wear your uniforms proudly, you shouldn't wear them at all until you learn how. I think you may learn how in two weeks."

Two weeks. Two weeks with Tinki San fighting off the whole damned United States Army and Marine Corps. I was dead. Pulverized. They should have buried me at sea.

We were all sitting on the fantail, near the garbage cans, when Frank came up with the idea. He casually lit a cigarette and sent the match arcing over the side of the ship.

"Look," he said, "we can't just sit around for two weeks. We'll go batty."

Mike agreed. "It's only been three days, and I'm already set for Section Eight," he said.

"All right," Frank said. He shifted his enormous buttocks on the ammo locker, drew in on his cigarette. "We got to do something, then."

"Sure," I said, "but what?"

"This ship is like a ghost tanker," Jack said. "I never knew so many guys went ashore at the same time."

"That's exactly it," Frank agreed enthusiastically. "There's only one answer."

"What's that?" Jack asked.

"Pinochle."

"Huh?"

"Pinochle," Frank repeated.

I shrugged. "What's Pinochle?" I asked.

"That's a card game," Mike put in.

"I don't know how to play it," Jack said.

"Don't you play cards?"

"Sure," Jack said hastily, slightly miffed by Frank's

accusation. *"Knuckles,* and *Steal the Old Man's Pack."* He paused, then added, "Other games, too."

Mike slapped his hand against his forehead. "Brother!"

"I don't know how to play Pinochle, either," I confessed.

Frank seemed to consider this for a few moments. His eyes looked out over the horizon, over to the camouflaged Jap buildings on the shore line. After a while, he flicked his cigarette into the water, and it made a faint *hiss* when it hit the surface. "We'll teach you," he said.

My eyes narrowed. "For fun?"

Frank looked hurt. "Why, sure! You think I want your money? We're all in this together, mate. I'm just looking to kill a little time."

"Sounds all right," Jack said. He was looking wistfully toward the shoreline.

"Let's get a blanket then," Mike said. "We can stretch out on the boat-deck, just aft of the forward stack."

"Sure," I agreed. I went down to the compartment for a blanket.

They explained the game to us, and it was really simple. A king and a queen are a marriage. Ten, Jack, Queen, King, Ace are a book—or a run, as it's sometimes called. Jack of diamonds and Queen of spades is a Pinochle. Then there's Forty Jacks, Sixty Queens, Eighty Kings, and a Hundred Aces. Simple.

It was a lot of fun, and Jack and I caught on pretty fast. We played opposite Frank and Mike, and after only one day of play, Frank said, "You guys are bidding like masters already."

I thought so, too, and my chest kind of swelled inside my tee shirt as we played. We kept winning, game after game, and Frank seemed to be getting a little sore about it. After all, he'd just taught us the game, and here we were paddling his britches.

Jack and I played a particularly brilliant hand, and Frank tossed his cards onto the blanket. He leaned back against the stack and said, "I quit!"

I was a little shocked. I looked at Jack, and he looked at me, and then we both looked at Frank. "Why?" I asked.

"There's no fun," Frank complained. "You guys keep winning all the time, and I'm beginning to lose interest."

"Well, gee," I said, "we won't *always* win."

"It's beginning to look that way," Mike said.

"Just the ways the cards are running," Jack told him.

"Yeah." There was defeat in Mike's voice.

"What's the sense of playing and losing all the time?" Frank asked. "Hell, I'm getting so I don't even want to pick up the next hand."

I shook my head. "Well, that's that, I guess."

"If only we could find a way to make it more interesting," Mike said.

"Sure," Frank agreed, "but how?"

"We could play for money," Mike suggested.

"What? You think I'm crazy? These guys are hotter than the rear stack. You think I'm a philanthropist?"

"What's that, Frank?" Jack wanted to know.

"You think I'm Santa Claus?" Frank clarified.

"We couldn't play for money, anyway," I reminded them. "That's against regulations."

"We could get around that," Mike said.

"How?" Frank sounded reluctantly dubious.

"We could keep the number of games won and lost in a little book—or on a piece of paper. How would anyone know we were playing for money?"

"Count me out," Frank said. "These guys are too hot."

"We can play for Jap money," Mike said. "That'd make it interesting, and we can always get plenty of that for cigarettes when we finally do go ashore."

"Well . . . maybe," Frank said.

"I don't think we should play for money," I put in. "It's against regulations."

"Heck," Jack said, "you can hardly call these *yens* money, Bob."

"It's money to the Japs," I answered.

"Yeah, but we ain't Japs," Mike said.

"I'm still not sure I want to play," Frank said.

"Aw, come on," Jack cajoled.

"Well, if Bob plays, I'll play," Frank said.

I thought about Tinki San again, and how the card games had taken my mind off her. Then I shrugged my shoulders.

"All right. But let's keep the stakes low."

"Radarman Striker Bishop report to the quarterdeck," a loudspeaker blared. "On the double."

Frank got to his feet slowly. "Wonder what those simple bastards want now?" he asked of no one in particular. We watched him amble off slowly. It turned out he was being called to relieve the fire watch, so we never did get to play anymore that day.

The entire crew aired its bedding on Tuesday, and the ship looked like a floating whore house, with mattresses everywhere you looked. At 1300, every guy and his brother made for the quarterdeck, all dressed in pretty blues. They collected their liberty cards and climbed down the ladder into the waiting launch. Practically the only things left on the ship were the mattresses and the four of us.

We grabbed a mattress with the name Richard S. Brown stencilled on both ends, and dragged it behind the aft stack.

"Who's this guy Brown?" Frank asked.

"Who knows?" Mike shrugged.

"I think he's a ping jockey," Jack said.

"He won't miss it," Frank said. "This airing never helps, anyway. They stink just as much when you drag them belowdecks."

"Well, are we playing for *yen* or not?" Mike asked.

"I guess so," I said.

Mike shuffled the cards and dealt, and we picked up our hands.

"Shall we make it twenty *yen* a game?" Mike asked.

"That's too steep," Frank said.

"All right. Fifteen, then."

"That sounds okay."

"Okay with me," Jack said.

"Fifteen," I agreed.

Jack and I won the first two games, and Mike marked them down in a little black book. He and Frank took the third game, and then Jack and I took the next four.

"This is gonna buy a lot of Chop Suey," Jack said. He was beaming happily as he looked at the figures Mike wrote in the book. I was figuring on buying Tinki San a nice string of beads, or maybe a silk kimono. I realized, of course, that I could've gotten the same kind of money by taking four packs of cigarettes ashore. For a carton of butts, you could have bought the island of Kyushu. In fact, they probably would have thrown in Honshu and the Emperor's palace.

"You're not going to be lucky all the time," Frank complained.

"Why don't we raise the stakes?" Jack asked.

"Oh no," Mike said.

"Why not?" Jack countered. "We're not going to be lucky all the time."

A large swell passed under the ship and we bobbed pleasantly on the water. Overhead, a crowd of seagulls cawed noisily. They were probably waiting for us to dump our garbage.

Frank seemed to concentrate on the gulls as he spoke. "All right, we'll up the stakes. But no more than twenty *yen* a hand."

"Suits me," Jack said, a broad smile on his face.

Mike dug into his wallet and came up with a few large, flimsy bills which he placed on the mattress. "I'm almost out of this crap," he said. He stuffed them back into his wallet.

Jack dealt the cards around, and the bidding started. Frank took the bid for two-hundred, and melded about a hundred-twenty. Mike's meld brought the total up to a hundred-sixty, and then we began to play. With forty points to go, you'd think they'd have made it easily. But we dumped them, and Frank blew his stack at Mike.

"Where the hell did you learn to play cards?" he asked. "Forty lousy points! We should have made that in two tricks."

"I just didn't have the cards," Mike said.

"You haven't got any brains, either."

"I haven't got any more *yen*, either," he said, "now that you mention it."

"Well, then let's square up and call it quits," Frank said.

"Suits me fine," Jack put in.

"It should suit you," Frank said. "You've cleaned us both."

We went down to the compartment and they paid off according to the figures in the book, Mike paying me, and Frank paying Jack. Then we went topside again and sat around near the forward gun turret, the big twin five-inchers pointing out at the sky, the gun bloomers a deep blue against the grey of the turret.

It was still early, and a quiet calm hung over the harbor. The water was a bright blue, and it rolled lazily, lifting the ship and dropping her again with simple ease. We lay stretched out on the deck, watching the wide expanse of sky, cloudless now, an endless stretch of blue wash overhead.

"Christ, this is dull," Frank said.

"Yeah."

"I understand this town is wide open, too. That god-damn SP. If I ever meet him without his armband . . ."

"He's probably a permanent Shore Patrol," Jack said. "Attached to the base, you know."

"He won't be so permanent if I ever catch up with him," Mike said, repeating Frank's sentiments.

We kept shooting the breeze, and then Frank said, "Christ, this is dull."

"You already said that," Jack reminded him.

"I know. And it's still dull. Let's play some more cards."

"I'm broke," Mike said.

"*Yen*, you mean?"

"Yeah."

"Let's play for dollars, then," Frank suggested.

Mike hesitated. "All right," he said at last. Jack agreed enthusiastically. Heck, this was money in the bank as far as he was concerned. Even I went along. We'd been lucky so far, and I was beginning to believe we were just more skillful than either Mike or Frank. And who can't use

more money? So we went back to Richard S. Brown's—
whoever he was—mattress, and started playing again,
with the stakes at a dollar a man each game.

And that's when Jack and I started losing.

It was uncanny, really. Frank and Mike suddenly got
hot, just like that, and they began to click immediately.
They played as if they were reading each other's minds,
as if the cards had suddenly become alive for them.

In the first game, Frank bid all the way up to three-
fifty, with Jack playing it real cute and upping the bid
when he didn't have beans in his hand. We figured that
we had them over a barrel with that three-fifty bid, and
then Frank melded a book for two-fifty, and a hundred
Aces, and they won the hand without having to play a
card.

In the second game, they gave us the bid for a paltry
two-twenty-five, and then exhibited a dazzling burst of
playing that dumped us flat on our backs even though
we'd melded one-sixty.

Jack tried to laugh it off, and soon we were well into
the sixth game, and we hadn't copped a single one. I was
beginning to get a little nervous because it was a long way
to payday, and I like the long green stuff a lot. We hit the
tenth game and lost that in about four minutes flat, and
Mike kept writing in his little book, and all the marks
were under his name and Frank's.

Jack was getting a little desperate by this time, I could
see. He wiped his hand over his upper lip and said, "Let's
do it this time, Bob. We're just in a slump."

I agreed with him because I couldn't understand how
our luck could have changed so radically. So we tried for
another five games, and we won one of those, with the

other four being chalked up to Frank and Mike, and with us owing them thirteen bucks after fifteen games.

We should have quit right then, I guess. But when you're thirteen bucks in the hole, you figure you've got a little bit invested in the game, if you know what I mean. If you pack up and go, you're out thirteen and that's that.

So we stuck around while Frank and Mike joked and had one hell of a big time. They were winning now, and it was Uncle Sugar's currency and not money you could buy with cigarettes. We stuck around, all right, and they clipped us for another fourteen bucks apiece, and when we finally went down to chow, we each owed twenty-seven bucks—and that ain't hay when you're a Seaman First Class, bucking for a petty officer's stripe.

After chow, Jack and I watched the movie, sitting high up on the Sugar Mike antenna mast and looking down at the screen.

When they stopped to change reels, Jack nudged me and I looked at his face, the round features lighted by the moon overhead.

"They're really taking us," he said.

"They've really *took* us," I corrected. "That's all for me. No more. Finis. End."

"You're gonna let them walk off with twenty-seven bucks?" Jack asked, his voice incredulous.

"We got off easy," I said. "If we keep playing, they're liable to walk off with our pay for the next year—and they'll probably wind up with our dress blues to boot."

"They just hit a lucky streak," Jack said. "We can make a comeback."

"*You* can make a comeback," I corrected again. "Get another partner. I've lost enough, thanks."

"I got a plan," Jack said.

The ship rolled a little, and I tightened my grip on the platform under the antenna. It was a long drop to the deck.

"What kind of a plan?"

"A plan so we can get back that dough. We can quit after we do that."

"What's your plan?" I asked. The movie had started again, but we weren't watching it now. Far down below us, the water lapped against the steel sides of the ship, and little fluorescent flashes of light winked up at us from the calm surface of the harbour.

"Look," Jack said, his voice lowering, "the whole trick to this game is the bidding, right?"

"Right."

"Okay. So let's take an example. Let's suppose I know you're strong in hearts. You bid two-hundred, then Mike bids, and then the bid comes to me. Let's say I've got a nice heart hand, too. I'll boost the bid all the way up, and we can't lose. Or suppose I ain't got hearts but I'm strong in spades. So I'll bid and you can check your hand for spades. You follow me? We won't be playing blind."

"Yeah, but how're we gonna know what we got in each other's hands?"

"Well, that's my plan."

"Lemmee hear it."

"We'll work it alphabetically. Clubs, diamonds, hearts, spades. One finger is clubs, two is diamonds, three is hearts, and four is spades."

"You mean we're gonna hold up fingers?"

"No, no. When we're holding the cards in our hands, we'll rest the fingers on our right hands against the backs of the cards. One will be clubs, two . . ."

"That's cheating," I said.

Jack looked hurt. "Whattya mean cheating?"

"What you said. Tipping each other's hands. That's cheating."

"It ain't cheating," Jack said. "And besides, we're losing twenty-seven bucks."

I nodded my head in the darkness. "Yeah," I agreed, "maybe it ain't cheating."

We started playing again the next day, right after the crew left on liberty. It was drizzling slightly, so we played down in the compartment on one of the foot lockers. We had it all planned, and we'd even practiced putting our fingers on the cards so that the other guy could read the hand without any trouble.

Mike dealt the first hand, and while he was dealing, Jack asked, "How about doubling the stakes, boys?"

Frank smiled. "You feeling hot again, Jack?"

Jack winked at me and said, "No, just figured we'd make it a little more interesting."

"I think we'd better leave the stakes as they are," Frank said.

"Why not up them?" I asked, trying to sound innocent, and feeling guilty as hell.

Frank shrugged. "Okay, if you say so. I don't like to make this a cutthroat game, though. I like it to be friendly."

Jack smiled, and I saw that he'd already picked up all his cards. I looked across and saw two fingers resting across the complicated bicycle design on the backs of the cards. Two fingers: diamonds. I checked through my own hand and saw that I had three diamonds, including an Ace. Quickly, I put two fingers across the back of my cards. Jack grinned and the bidding began.

"Two-hundred," Jack said.

"Two-fifty," Mike followed.

"Two-seventy-five," I said. I didn't want to bump it too soon. I didn't want them to get suspicious.

"Three," Frank said.

"Three-twenty," from Jack.

"Three-fifty," from Mike.

I looked at my hand again. The bidding was getting kind of steep. I looked over at Jack again, and saw the two fingers as big as life. Two fingers: diamonds.

"Three-sixty," I said cautiously.

"Three-seventy," Frank bid.

"Three-eighty," Jack said without hesitation.

Mike paused and looked at his cards again, then stroked his long lantern jaw. "Three-ninety."

"Make it four," I said.

"Pass."

"Pass."

"Pass."

"I guess it's ours, Bob," Jack said happily. We started melding, and our total came to two-fifty, with Jack melding a book in diamonds. We had a hundred and fifty to go to make the bid, and we had eight diamonds, and they, of course, were trumps.

Yeah, well don't ask me how we fluffed it. All I know is that we were out of diamonds before you could say "Jack Robinson," and then Frank and Mike began pulling in tricks hand over fist. We wound up with three-eighty, twenty points shy of what we'd bid, and Mike chalked up another game for himself and his partner. Jack and I really buckled down, and we flashed our signal fingers like crazy, but before the Officer of the Day stumbled into the compartment, we'd lost another ten games and were now forty-seven bucks in the hole, what with Jack and his brilliant "double-stakes" idea. The OD broke up the game and warned us about playing for money. When we told him there was no money involved, he whispered a four letter word attesting to the truthfulness of our statement and then left, warning us once more.

Mike picked up the cards and stacked them neatly. Then he put them into their box, and stuffed the box into the back pocket of his dungarees. He left, and Frank sat around and shot the breeze awhile before he, too, went topside. I just stared at Jack for about five minutes.

"What happened?" I asked at length.

Jack shrugged. "I don't know."

"We'd better work out another system," I said.

"Yeah," he whispered. "Honesty is the best policy."

"In a pig's ear," I told him. Then we put our heads together and worked out an elaborate system of eye-twitching, nose-rubbing, elbow-scratching, button-pulling, cigarette-lighting, teeth-showing, sneezing, coughing, stuttering, smiling, laughing gestures through which we could telegraph every card we held in our hands. We spent the rest of the day memorizing the signals, and that night we sat on the boat deck under the stars and went over them once more. There was a signal for every card in the deck, and we kept the "fingers" method to establish suit. We were ready to win back our forty-seven bucks and call it quits.

The game started at 1600 the next day, right after Mike came off watch. We had the blanket all set up when he got there, and Frank had already dealt the cards.

Jack picked up his hand and twitched his left eye while he put one finger on the cards in his hand. Nine of clubs.

He tugged at the first button on his shirt and flashed two fingers. Ace of diamonds. He smiled and flashed one finger again. Jack of clubs. He went on like this while I studied his hand and tried to memorize the cards. Then I began flashing my hand, and before we were done, we had a pretty good idea of what we both held.

The bidding started, and Frank took it for two-fifty. We played the hand out, and I knew every card Jack was throwing before he even threw it. We won the first game.

We started another game, and it was a close one, with Frank and Mike finally taking it.

Jack and I took the third game.

Frank and Mike took the fourth and fifth, and then we took the sixth.

We took the seventh.

Frank and Mike took the eighth.

Frank was beginning to sweat as we started the ninth game. He picked up his cards and looked over at Mike's hand, and his eyes shifted to my cards as I busily twitched and coughed and grinned and counted buttons while telegraphing my hand to Jack.

"Can't seem to get started today," Frank complained.

"Yeah," Jack admitted, a puzzled frown on his face. "Pretty tight."

The bidding began, and Mike took it this time for three-twenty. And then we started to play. It was tight all right. Each man studied his cards carefully before discarding. We'd gone about ten minutes, I think, before twelve cards had been played.

I led off with a nine of diamonds, and Frank topped it with a Queen. I looked over at Jack, and he seemed to hesitate a minute. I rubbed my nose and hoped he understood I wanted him to throw his King. He still hesitated, so I rubbed my nose again.

"Come on," Frank said impatiently.

Jack put down a ten of diamonds, and my eyes opened wide in disbelief. "Your King!" I shouted. "What's the matter with your King?"

Frank leaped to his feet, upsetting the locker top we had across our knees and scattering the cards onto the deck.

"I thought so!" he bellowed. "You lousy bastards have been reading the cards too."

I didn't know what he meant at first, and before I could say anything, he'd hooked his big paw into my shirt front and was pulling me off my feet.

"Reading the cards?" Jack shouted. "You mean these cards are marked?"

Frank looked at Jack, and his face turned white as he realized he'd pulled a blunder. His fingers relaxed in my shirt, but this time *I* was sore. The bastards had been playing with marked cards all along—taking our money. The bastards had been cheating!

I tossed my fist into Frank's face and he came charging back at me, two hundred pounds of enraged bull. Mike piled on, and then Jack was alongside me pounding away and cards were all over the place and the ship rocked with our violent movement.

The Officer of the Day finally broke us up, but not before I'd torn Mike's little black book into a thousand small pieces.

The old man tossed us all into the brig, on bread and water, just the way he'd promised. He said that uniform of the day on the U.S.S. *Bessemer* was dungarees and white hats. When the OD broke us apart, Frank's pants had been ripped almost completely off, Mike's shirt had only one sleeve, Jack was standing in his shorts, and my tee shirt was in ribbons. The old man said we were out of uniform, and I guess maybe he was right.

They put us all in the same cell, and we've rigged up a little candle in the center of the deck. We sit around it all day and play cards. The cards aren't marked. I know, because we made them by tearing twenty-six *yen* notes in half and writing numbers and suits on them. Playing cards occupies the time. Two weeks in the brig can get mighty dull otherwise.

We don't play Pinochle, though. We've been playing a game Jack taught us. It's called *Go Fish*.

S.P.Q.R.

SAM EPMAN was a short man with a bald head and a mustache that looked as if it were experimental and impermanent. The transitory appearance of the mustache was perhaps caused by two coinciding phenomena, one completely natural, the other induced by the fine hand of Epman himself.

On nature's side the otherwise black mustache was liberally sprinkled with gray which, rather than giving it that highly touted "distinguished" look, simply created an impression of sparseness, of unhairy patches scattered throughout the black. Left to its own devices, nature might have triumphed over the odd coloration, but it was here that Epman entered the picture. Unaware of the optical illusion, Epman unwittingly added to the natural effect by keeping the broad mustache trimmed very close to his lip. The total effect was something less than rewarding. You could assume that Epman had rubbed a grimy finger under his nose, or you could in equal error assume he'd begun growing the unsightly lip piece only the day before yesterday.

To make matters worse, Epman constantly called the mustache to the attention of anyone who happened to be in its vicinity. In the middle of a conversation his fingers would reach up suddenly and spasmodically to smooth a mustache that needed no smoothing whatever. Thumb would stroke one end of the short-bristled smear, forefinger frantically working on the other end. Sam Epman became a colonel of Indian cavalry, briskly stroking, smoothing, caressing a nonexistent handle-bar mustache.

The hand would move fitfully in a downward motion as if desperately trying to control this wild hairy growth, as if anxious to merge mustache with mouth.

At four o'clock that afternoon, with the rain having dwindled to a slow, steady drizzle, with the Roman sun feebly attempting to poke its way through the persistent overhang, Sam Epman stood before the long window in his suite and briskly stroked his mustache as he introduced me to Peter Wainwright. A sunless glare limned Epman's body so that his face remained a blur from which radiated only the blinking reflection of the pinky diamond on his left hand.

"I'm always surprised when two top writers don't know each other," he said, smiling, the stroking hand suddenly dropping to his vest where one thumb automatically hooked itself into a pocket. "Any other business, the top people in it usually know each other, if not intimately at least to say hello to. You manufacture cap pistols—don't it stand to reason you should know the competition? Even Gimbels knows Macy's. So what is it with writing and writers?"

Epman's blue eyes twinkled as if he were about to reveal the secret of birth to a pair of atheistic obstetricians. The eyes were overhung with thick, unruly black eyebrows that seemed determined to compensate for the lack of hair on his head and the sparse look of his mustache. The brows would have been menacing were it not for the warmth of the blue eyes. It was, perhaps, the eyes that had first convinced me there might be some worth in a project which seemed patently ridiculous on the surface.

"With writers there's no real competition," Epman explained, pleased with his analysis. "Writing is the one business—pro*fession,* excuse me—where it don't matter how many best sellers there are. Does it hurt David Cohen the people should also be buying a book by Peter Wainwright? This ain't like a cap pistol where you got one you don't need another. Books you always need. In fact, you read one good one, it makes you want to run out and buy another one. So there's no real competition. Oh, yes, maybe it burns you up a little some other writer's book is number three when your book is only number four, but there's no *real* competition; you write the best book you know how and then you leave it to God. You don't have to get out there and fight with your teeth and your nails to hang onto whatever little piece of the earth you finally managed to get."

Epman's hand leaped from the vest pocket, violently stroked the end of the mustache, and then fluttered down again.

"So with no competition, it ain't necessary you should know other writers. In fact, it's a little bit of a pain in the ass. What do writers want to talk about? Writing, what else? So it's supposed to be fun to listen to another writer tell you all about his new plot? This is fun?" He shook his head. "Writers avoid other writers. Oh, they know a few, yes. This is only to keep up appearances, people shouldn't say they're anti-social. But how many dentists do you think have friends who ain't in the dental profession? Maybe three or four, and they're already old *cockuhs* who are ready to drop dead. Dentists stick with dentists, doctors stick with doctors, pimps even they stick with other pimps. Writers, their best friends are their typewriters."

Sam Epman smiled. He had a wide mouth which, when possessed by a smile, seemed to claim his entire face. "So," he said, "David Cohen, meet Peter Wainwright." He smiled again. "You're both so talented, when you shake hands short stories should come popping out of your ears."

Wainwright and I, prompted by Epman's cue, shook hands, but nothing popped out of our ears. Wainwright was wearing a black suit and a black tie, and he gave a tailored impression of a man honed to knife-edge perfection. Dark suit, dark hair, dark eyes, I thought, a cautious smile and a firm handclasp, first impressions of Peter Wainwright.

"Glad to meet you, Dave," Wainwright said, and I added to the impression a deep, well-modulated voice and a person who immediately placed a total stranger on a first-name basis. "I read your book. It's an excellent job."

"Thank you," I answered. I could not say I had read or enjoyed any of his books because I'd never been tempted to crack a single one of them. Nor could I bring myself to call this dark, lean stranger Peter or Pete or Petey or, in the face of his earlier familiarity, even Mr. Wainwright. Feeling completely inadequate, I settled for the two words "Thank you" and a manly handclasp and hoped I appeared neither foolish nor aloof.

"I got the title for the picture," Epman said suddenly, interrupting a handshaking scene that was becoming awkwardly incessant. "You remember when I talked to you at the Waldorf in New York, I didn't have a title. Then I only knew I wanted to do *Julius Caesar,* but I also knew *Julius Caesar* we couldn't call it. If you bring *Julius Caesar* up to date, you don't still call it *Julius Caesar,* do you? You also don't call it *Big Julie* or something like that. This is the one thing you don't call it. This picture has got to have class, so you don't start with Hollywood craperoo. I know Hollywood craperoo from the time I was eighteen years old and running inter-office memos for Irving Thalberg."

"Did you work with Thalberg?" Wainwright asked in his deep, well-modulated voice. He leaned forward in expectant interest, his brown eyes alert in his narrow face, his brows raised in anticipation.

"I worked with all of them. You name them, I worked with them. All the big producers, the directors, the stars, you name them and I worked with them. You talk about competition—the picture business got competition like the World Series." His hand came up to stroke the mustache. "But I'm still alive and kicking, thank God, and I got enough dough to be an independent and to pay the talent I need to make a class movie. Gentlemen, this picture ain't going to be a Metro musical or a Warner Brothers gangster epic, and it ain't going to be either a thing where some smart jerk buys a best seller and then hires a screen hack for fifteen hundred bucks a week he should louse up the story by sticking in it original ideas he never had in his life. This is going to be class, which is why I hired talents, not hacks, talents who are capable of thinking original, who can take a play like Shakespeare's *Julius Caesar* which has withstood the test of time for what —three centuries?—take this play and translate it into English which the average movie-goer, Mr. and Mrs. America, can understand without we have to put titles on the bottom of the picture to translate from the blank verse."

I glanced at Wainwright, but he seemed completely absorbed by what Epman was saying. I felt again the twinge I'd first felt at the Waldorf last month when Epman initially outlined the project.

"Did Shakespeare write in Latin?" Epman asked now,

as he had asked that day last month in his Waldorf suite. "No, he wrote in Elizabethan blank verse, and the people who watched his plays were used to listening to this blank verse and to understanding it. This was a language that was immediately understood by the crowd that had come to the Globe Theatre to be entertained. So Shakespeare entertained them. He stole these solid plots from sources God knows where he found them, from Plutarch, from Thomas Lodge, from Fiorentino—anybody who ever put a good story on paper, Shakespeare swiped it. In those days there were no copyright laws, gentlemen, he saw something he liked, he grabbed it. The son of a bitch never had an original plot all the time he was living. And he took these plots and wrote this glorious poetry around them, but is it the blank verse that plays today, or is it the construction of the plays, the fire they've got underneath all that poetry? I'll tell you what it is."

Sam Epman lighted a cigar and passed the box around. Both Wainwright and I refused. Sucking on the cigar, Epman said "It's the story. Story, that's the secret. Poetry is great for English literature courses; am I trying to take away from this glorious poetry the man wrote? But poetry don't sell tickets. In Elizabethan times, yes, it sold tickets because it was the language they understood. Today the people don't understand it. It detracts from the play; it detracts from the psychological penetration this man Shakespeare had. It detracts, to put it in terms you writers understand, it detracts from the universality.

"What the hell is *Julius Caesar* if not universal? What is this, the story of a dictator? The story of a band of patriots? Baloney! This is the story of a power grab, that's what this is the story of. You can set this story in a New England factory town, and it will still play. Why? Because man has been concerned with power from the minute he discovered he could hit another man on the head with a club and take away his woman and the saber-toothed rug from his cave. Power and success, what the hell is *Julius Caesar* all about if not that? And what is life today all about if not power and success? Today there's no cavemen to kill. Today you got to kill some son-of-a-bitch account executive. Today, when you make your grab, you don't get Gaul; you get maybe the right to tell people how mild Chesterfield cigarettes are, but this is a piece of the world, this is what buys you that Cadillac or that Mercedes, this is what puts that luscious blonde on your arm, this is what pays for those hand-tailored suits. Don't kid yourselves, it's the same today as it was then. Today you don't use daggers; you use words and smiles, but you're bucking for the same thing: *power!* And you can equate that with success, and that's where we grab Mr. and Mrs. America by the genitals, because success or failure, power or lack of power is something they live with every day of their lives."

Sam Epman began pacing the rug-covered floor of his suite, a short bald man wearing a gray tropical suit and bright green slipper socks. He sucked interminably on his cigar, leaving a trail of agitated smoke behind him.

"So what's our movie all about? Our movie is all about power. And we are going to tell our story of power in modern, everyday, *American* English. We are going to tell this story of a political assassination in terms every citizen of the United States will be able to understand. We are going to keep the old Roman setting, and the same situation, but we are going to relate this tale of a power grab so that there will be no mistake about it. We are going to tell it so that everybody seeing this first-rate motion picture will understand that it applies to their lives today, now, this minute, we are still assassinating people in our grabs for power, does that make sense?"

"It seems to make a lot of sense," Wainwright said quietly.

Epman turned to face me, and I nodded quickly.

"You want to know the title?" Epman said. "This is the title—hold your hats. The title is S.P.Q.R." He paused for effect. Wainwright and I stared at him blankly. "Does it mean anything to you?"

"Is it a cryptogram?" Wainwright asked.

"No, it ain't a cryptogram, but it has mystery, you got to admit that. It also has six-foot-high letters we can spread across a Cinemascope screen one letter at a time, S . . ." He wrote the letter in the air with his cigar. ". . . . P . . . Q . . . R . . . can you see those letters materializing on the screen? S.P.Q.R., with the triumphal music of ancient Rome in the background, starring Burt Lancaster or whoever, superimposed over a reconstruction of old Rome, a Roman street teeming with life, jumping right into those opening lines of—"

"Do you think you can get Lancaster?" Wainwright interrupted.

Epman waved the interruption aside impatiently. "Lancaster, Shmancaster," he said, "who cares what star we get, a star we'll get, a whole bunch of stars we'll get, don't worry. What the hell are actors but instruments a director blows on them and he gets from them the music *you* wrote? You got money, you get stars. Only in astronomy are stars life-giving suns. In real life stars are only a fiction we made up to keep the people happy. These are the Roman gods and goddesses of today, only we don't erect statues of them, we make celluloid pictures instead. Don't bother me with stars, stars we'll get by the bushelful. How do you like the title?"

"It sounds impressive," Wainwright said, "but I don't know what it means."

"Your first day in Rome, you ain't supposed to know what it means yet. That's why you're here, to dig around, to get the feel. How you going to write about Rome if you ain't got the feel of it? Wouldn't it be cheaper if I kept you in New York instead of *shlepping* you all the way over here? But this is what's going to give the picture class, ancient Rome right down to the last detail, but the actors speaking English we can all understand." He turned to me. "You know what S.P.Q.R. means?"

"No," I admitted.

"It means *Senatus Populusque Romanus.* And in English that means 'The Senate and People of Rome,' and it was stamped on government property all over the city in ancient Roman times, and you can still see it all over Rome today. S.P.Q.R."

"Was it used during Caesar's time?" I asked.

"I don't know, and I don't give a damn. I guess it was. If it wasn't, we'll stretch a point, because I ain't going to throw away an excellent title just because Julius Caesar didn't happen to think of it." He paused. "So? How do you like it?"

"I'm not sure," Wainwright said cautiously. "It may be a little too esoteric for the common man."

"Those are two words I don't know the meaning of," Epman said. "Esoteric and common man. The common man knows only what you throw at him in the advertisements. We take a full-page ad in the New York *Times,* and the ad on one side has these big black letters S.P.Q.R. and on the other side running down the full length of the page, this babe in a Roman toga—she's supposed to be Cal-purnia. The toga is cut down to her navel in the front, and you can see her whole leg right up past her thigh where the toga is slit on the side. The common man he don't wonder any more what S.P.Q.R. spells. The common man takes one look at the half-naked babe, and he knows right away that S.P.Q.R. spells SEX.

"You take out the same ad the next day, only on the right-hand side, instead of the babe, you got a guy stab-bing another guy in a toga, and the common man figures out that S.P.Q.R. spells VIOLENCE. There ain't nothing common about the common man except his reactions. The only thing that scares him is class, because he ain't sure what it is. So to give him class, you got to make believe it's crap. After a while, when he begins to think class is really crap—which he understands—he feels comfortable. S.P.Q.R. is a classy title, believe me."

Epman paused.

"What's so great about a title like *From Here to Eternity,* would you mind telling me? It sounds like may-be Norman Vincent Peale wrote it. You flash it across the screen—it's so long that half the people in the audience they fall asleep before they finish reading it. But all of a sudden it's a great title because it's attached to a success-ful property. Okay. One thing you can bet your life on. S.P.Q.R. is going to be a successful picture. It'll be the best damn picture I ever made, and believe me I made plenty. We don't gross forty million bucks on this one, I'll eat the shooting script." Epman chuckled and then studied the end of his cigar. "S.P.Q.R.," he said softly. "It's a good title. It'll become a magnificent title when it's attached to a success."

"There are many people," Wainwright said with that

same air of caution, "who feel that success is often pre-determined by the choice of a title."

"Well, all I got to say to those people is they're wrong," Epman answered. "Look at *Anatomy of a Murder*. That's a cockamamie title if ever I heard one, and they stick on the book a dust jacket it could make you puke. So what happens? It's a best seller for more than a year. You want to talk about titles, I could quote you titles don't even make sense and they were attached to some of the biggest properties ever came down the pike. What is *Gone with the Wind*? An inspiration? It makes you cry? It makes you laugh? Me, it makes me want to go out and buy an over-coat. What's *Lolita* all about? It sounds like the story of a Mexican flamenco dancer instead of a guy he leches for twelve-year-olds. Titles, don't start with titles. You want to know the secret of a title? I'll tell you. The best title in the world, it means absolutely nothing. It means a reader, an audience, they look at it and decide for themselves what it means. *That's* a title that says something. To say something it has to say absolutely nothing. And S.P.Q.R. doesn't say a goddamn thing." He paused. "Which is exactly why it says everything."

Epman blew out a wreath of smoke and then asked, "Am I right or am I right?" He seemed to be directing the question at me, but I was spared an answer by the sudden opening of the outer door to the suite. We all turned to face the door. Epman stroked his mustache.

"Sam, darling, would you help me with these packages, please?" a voice said, and I recognized the voice instantly as belonging to Flora Epman, the producer's wife. The voice emanated from a petite redhead in her fifties who, despite a barely noticeable thickening about the waist, was a living testament to what the slick magazines often

called The American Way of Life. Wearing a black
corduroy raincoat over a tan linen suit, beige pumps,
frilly white blouse showing at the throat of the suit jacket,
long red hair carefully rolled into a bun at the nape of the
neck, face and throat preserved through the magic of
countless applications of queen bee jelly, Flora struggled
into the room with her packages, and Epman hurried to
unburden her.

"Thank you, darling," she said, and one meticulously
manicured hand reached up to touch the bun at the back
of her neck, tidying it, the hand glistening with a diamond
the size of Quemoy. "Oh, gentlemen, I didn't realize you
were here. I hope I'm not interrupting anything. Oh, but
I *am*, aren't I? Forgive me. I'll be as quiet as a mouse."

"We were almost finished, Flora," Epman said. "You've
met both Mr. Cohen and Mr. Wainwright, haven't you?"

"Yes. You must forgive me, gentlemen. I know how
Sam is about his conferences. He can't even stand the
telephone intruding."

"Why, you've brought the sunshine with you, Mrs.
Epman," Wainwright said, smiling, and I glanced through
the window and noticed that the sun had indeed broken
through the clouds at last.

"Only to match your golden tongue," Flora answered
quickly with a look that seemed unconsciously flirtatious,
but only in a regal way, the smile a queen allows a sentry.
The look was curious because Flora Epman was not
beautiful, I realized, and yet she seemed to believe she
was beautiful, and her belief was contagious. "I must
change out of these wet clothes," she said.

"I was just telling them about the title, Flora," Epman
said. "S.P.Q.R."

"Yes, it's a good title, don't you think?" She took off the

wet black raincoat, pulled a hanger from the closet, and stopped on her way to the bathroom to face me.

"I don't know yet," I said. "It takes a while for a title to grow on me."

Flora went into the bathroom, apparently to hang the raincoat over the tub. She returned as Epman said, "It'll grow on you, don't worry. Even if it don't grow, it's a great title. On the common man, to use Mr. Wainwright's terminology, the only thing that grows on him is his toenails and his hair."

"But Mr. Cohen is not the common man," Flora said, smoothing the short suit jacket over her hips. "If he were, he wouldn't be working on this picture."

"Thank you," I said, and then wondered if I'd been complimented.

"I must change," Flora said. "I'm soaked through to my underwear." She smiled briefly and maternally, as if she hoped this inadvertent reference to her lacy unmentionables would not erect a lust-arousing image of herself. "Will you be long, Sam? I'd like to go downstairs for a cocktail."

"A few more minutes," Epman said. "You go ahead and change."

"If you'll excuse me," Flora said, and again she smiled and then moved toward the bathroom with a walk that was peculiarly unfeminine even though the hip and leg movements were those usually associated with feminine, if not outright sexy, women. The effect puzzled me. I watched her as she walked across the room. She was, I supposed, about five feet two inches tall. She walked with her shoulders back and her head erect, the bun at the nape of her neck curled with the artistic precision of a conch shell. Her waist, though beginning to record the advance of years, was slender nonetheless, smoothly flowing into the curve of wide hips. She moved with a fluidity that tightened her skirt across an invitingly plump backside, and her legs looked clean and trim, tapering to the flawlessly cut high-heeled pumps. The effect should have been one of desirable, if mellowing, femininity. And yet something was lacking.

She moves like a frightened bird, I thought.

I realized in a rush that Flora Epman had known either Hollywood or Sam Epman for too long a time. The marshmallow exterior she presented might once have been only the coating for a solid steel core, but it was genuine enough now. Whatever strength she'd once possessed had become a banality. For all her smiling agreement, she was a lost and frightened woman. And I wondered if Sam Epman hadn't made her that way.

Epman waited until the bathroom door had closed behind her.

"I'll make this short," he said. "You're the boys who are going to write this movie. Are you supposed to sit down and work with each other without even knowing what brand cigarettes you smoke? Impossible. I took the liberty," he went on, moving toward the dropleaf desk near the windows, lowering the front of the desk and reaching into it, "of buying copies of your respective books. Everybody should take such liberties, huh? Not that you need it." He chuckled. "Mr. Cohen, from you I bought *Slum Boy* because this is all you wrote so far. From you, Mr. Wainwright, I bought your latest one, *Tambourine*, on the theory that a man's latest is always his best." He picked up the books and carried them across the room. "You only get one book each," he said, chuckling. "Your own book you don't have to read." He extended the books. I took my copy. Wainwright glanced through his and then handed it back.

"I've already read this," he said.

"What?" Epman asked, as though he hadn't heard Wainwright's earlier praise of my novel.

"I thought it would be a good idea to research my colleague's work," Wainwright explained. He shrugged in embarrassment like a student who, in a class of forty, is the only one who's prepared his assignment.

"Well, good, good for you," Epman said. "But if you don't mind, would you read it again? I want you to get acquainted with each other's styles. We got to marry these two different styles into one shooting script; it shouldn't look like the Russian Army wrote it. So learn them. It won't be boring, believe me. Those are good books. If they weren't, their authors wouldn't be working on my picture."

He pulled a slender pocket watch from his vest pocket, held it on the palm of his hand for an instant, and then put it back into the pocket. "I'll see you all in the morning," he said. "In the meantime, I better get dressed or Flora will take a fit. Thanks for coming up."

"It was a pleasure hearing your ideas, Mr. Epman," Wainwright said. "It sounds as if we're going to have a great picture here."

"I think so," Epman said reflectively. "I think we're going to have a great picture here."

He paused and looked at me.

I cleared my throat. "I think we're going to have a great picture here," I said.

Epman smiled. Then, with sudden energy, he said, "Listen, I don't want you to think I'm kicking you out, because what I'm doing, actually, is kicking you out. Unless you want to see a hairy-legged producer in his undershorts." He chuckled and smoothed his mustache, as if mention of hair had reminded him of it. With his free hand he opened the door.

"See you in the morning, Mr. Epman," Wainwright said cheerfully.

"Right," Epman snapped with a curt nod of his bald head, and then he closed the door behind us. Wainwright and I stood awkwardly in the hallway.

"Feel like joining me for a drink, Dave?" he asked. He grinned. "Or would you rather start reading my novel?"

"The drink now, the novel later," I said.

We walked down the hallway in silence. I rang for the elevator, and then I turned to Wainwright, a frown on my face, and asked, "What do you think of all this? Do you think it'll really work?"

Wainwright nodded quickly. There was in his eyes the same fear I had felt emanating from Flora Epman. "I think it'll be a great picture," he said, and then as if I hadn't already done it, rang for the elevator again.

THE FINAL YES

HE TOOK THE KEY from his pocket, unlocked the padlock, and then took the shotgun down from the rack.

The shotgun was a Savage automatic, and he thought the name was wryly appropriate because he was about to kill himself and he considered the act essentially savage and at the same time automatic, almost inevitable. Holding the gun in his big hands, he looked down at it with a curiously sad smile. He hadn't even wanted the damn thing.

The house was very still.

He stood in the center of the wood-paneled den, alone in the house, the ceiling lights glinting on the sleek, polished barrel of the gun. His face in the shining barrel was eerily reflected, distorted by the curve of the metal and shimmer of the overhead fixture. The gun was light in his hands. It had a checkered walnut stock, with a full pistol grip. The barrel was plain and round, but it was made of a special alloy steel so that, even though it was a twelve-gauge gun, it felt as light as any twenty-gauge he'd ever handled. It was really ironic, he thought, that Beth was the one who'd insisted on buying the gun, over his protests. It was really so goddamn ironic that he felt like crying because . . . because this gun, this gun he held in his hands, was something more than a weapon or a deliverer. Its possession, his ownership of it even though he'd never wanted it, was an admission of a way of life. And his way of living had really left very little choice in determining the way of his dying.

How still the house was, almost as if it expected a

118

sudden noise and were bracing itself for the shock. That's ridiculous, he thought. The house is empty because Beth and the children are at the beach. No one expected me home this early, not on a Friday afternoon.

He looked at the gun again.

Well, he thought, I might as well get it over with. Shells, he thought. I suppose I'll need shells.

Aimlessly, he began walking toward the garage. The shotgun felt a little heavier in his hands. He felt no real sense of urgency, and yet he knew the thing had to be done before Beth and the children got home. He supposed that would be around five o'clock, and it was only three now. It seemed much later than that. The idea had come to him at exactly two-thirty, just a half hour ago. He had said his final "Yes" at that time and then had glanced at his desk clock, as if wanting to mark the hour, as if knowing even as the "Yes" left his lips that it was the last time he would ever say that word, the last time he would allow himself to be talked into doing something he did not want to do.

He found the box of shells at the back of one of the drawers in the old chest stored in the garage. He went back into the house and loaded the gun to its full five-shot capacity, even though he knew he'd need only one shot, and then he sat with the gun across his lap for several moments and tried to think if there was anything he wanted to do before he killed himself. He had no idea as yet whether he would put the barrel of the gun in his mouth or simply hold it against his temple. The idea of killing himself did not frighten him. In fact, he accepted it with a sort of depressive calm, as if he had known from the very beginning, from that time so long ago when he had first said "Yes," that this was the way it would end.

He decided to leave a note for Beth. He didn't really care whether or not she understood, but he felt nonetheless that he should leave some sort of note. He had given her little enough in her lifetime, and he didn't want her to think she was totally responsible for what he was going to do. Maybe she was partially responsible, but not entirely, and the least he could do for her was to leave a note to put her mind at ease.

He put the shotgun down on the floor alongside the desk, and he looked around in the desk drawer for a sheet of paper, closed the drawer, opened another one, reopened the first one, and found the pad right under his hand. He sharpened a pencil and then sat down in the desk chair and wondered what he could say to her and then thought, *The hell with her, let her figure it out herself,* and then relented, sighed, meticulously dated the top of the page, and wrote:

Dear Beth,
I'm not sure you will understand this. I'm not sure I understand it myself. I only know . . .

I'm not sure I do understand it, he thought. I'm really not sure I understand it at all. I only know that when Alan came into my office and put the question to me, when Alan asked me to do whatever it was he asked—I can hardly remember what he asked; it is only with a great effort of will that I can remember him asking at all—and I said, "Yes, sure, yes," I knew that was the end, I knew I had to do this.

He paused, holding the pencil poised over the pad, wondering how he could tell this to Beth. How do you explain to a woman you never loved the things that mean the most to you? How do you tell her about a boy who used to lie in bed beside a frost-rimmed window imagining a universe of ice-crystal stars stretching to eternity? How do you explain a boy who rolled up his trouser cuffs and waded in the river long before winter had released its grip, his toes numb, a foolish grin on his mouth? How do you explain the dreams of youth and the gradual disappearance of the dreams, of *any* dreams, until there was nothing left but a vast compromise with something only vaguely remembered? Where does it go? he wondered. How do you get to be forty-two years old and writing a farewell note to a woman you never wanted?

How can you tell her about a night that happened before she even existed, a night that happened before the beginning of time, when the lights of the ferris wheel traced a round-robin pattern against a starless sky? The calliope music was flooding the vacant lot upon which the carnival had pitched its travel-worn brown tents. There was the noise of barkers, and the simulated shrieking of young girls, and the mechanical roar of the amusement machines, and the tiny pop of the .22 in his hands, and the echoing sound of the bullets spanging against the gong at the far end of the gallery.

The girl was suddenly there.

He looked up as he reloaded the rifle, and the girl was there, and suddenly his hands were wet. She looked at him somewhat shyly, a tall girl of seventeen, with long blond hair and luminous brown eyes, a faint smile on her mouth. She was wearing a pale-blue cotton frock, and her legs were long and tanned, and she wore white sneakers dulled by the dust of the vacant lot. The night opened. The world dissolved. He looked at her, and everything he had ever wanted in all his long eighteen years was suddenly there, standing not three feet away from him. He put down the rifle. He looked at the girl soundlessly, and his eyes suddenly misted. And then, without expecting to, he held out his hand to her.

The girl looked at him curiously. She studied his face. she shook her head slightly and seemed about to speak, and then her eyes fastened to his, and the night narrowed into a single direct channel, the ferris wheel, the barkers, the terrified shrieks, the laughter, all melting beyond the fringes of focus, their eyes meeting and holding with an intensity so great it excluded all else. Speechless, she took his hand.

The carnival was a part of the dream. They walked through its tinsel and glitter like figures from another time, displaced. There was a glow of unreality to the night. The lights seemed softer now, the music indistinct, the laughter muffled and far away. Only the girl was real, and even the girl was part of the dream. She would not tell him her name. They made a game of it, he trying to guess, and she repeatedly shaking her head, her laughter rising to join the music of the calliope. He bought her a jelly apple, and he watched, bewitched, as her teeth sank into the thick candy crust, and he said, "Your name is Guinevere."

"No."

"Elaine then?"

"No."

Her laughter. Walking with a gentle, delicate step, the dust-covered sneakers carrying her gracefully over the lot and then to the littered sidewalk beyond, and across the town to where the river snaked in unreflecting blackness, overhung with the willows on its bank. He held her hand and guided her to the water's edge. The grass was wet with dew. He cupped her face in one hand and whispered, "Tell me your name."

"My name is the wind," she said, and laughed.

"Tell me."

"I wish you would kiss me," she said. "Please kiss me."

Still holding her face, feeling the hard line of her jaw beneath his fingers, he lowered his mouth, and her lips parted, and he closed his eyes and held her very tight. In that instant all the romantic visions of his youth, all the fantasies he had drawn on the nighttime ceiling of his room, the imagined legends of tall, gallant men and beautiful, delicate maidens, came alive in this girl whose name he did not know. The willows hung like teardrops caught by time.

And with this girl, with this gentle girl who lay softly cradled in his arms by the edge of the river, there came purpose and resolve. He was suddenly brimming with plans; ambition rose within him like a tower. Holding her in his arms, he spun a golden thread of reveries, whispering lest the night be shattered by sound, until at last she sighed and said, "I must go."

"I'll take you home," he said softly. "Where do you live?"

"I live in the air," she answered, and again she laughed.

"No, seriously."

"I'll find my way alone. I want you to stay here."

"I want to come with you," he said, puzzled.

"Kiss me again."

He held her to him and kissed her again, but there was an unfamiliar panic rising within him. He did not want to let her go. Fiercely he clung to her.

"Don't go yet," he said. "Please."

"I'm going. I must."

"No. Please . . ."

"Do you love me?" she asked suddenly.

"Yes, but . . ."

"Then love me," she said, "and let me go."

He was frightened all at once. Suddenly he was afraid that if he insisted he would lose her completely. He nodded bleakly in the darkness. "Yes," he said. "All right."

She rose and brushed her skirt, her long, thin fingers moving silently in the darkness.

"Will I see you tomorrow?" he asked.

"Yes, tomorrow," she said.

"Here?"

"Tomorrow," she said.

She kissed him suddenly and swiftly and then slipped out of his arms and ran up the grassy bank. He could hear her laughter trailing behind her.

"I love you!" he called to the night.

She did not come the next day. He waited until it was dark, and then beyond that, and then he simply sat on the river's edge, no longer waiting, and stared deep into the black waters.

He looked for her all that summer.

The songs they were playing in 1937 helped to perpetuate the dreamlike quality of that night by the river. Every note he heard echoed of faraway places, any one of which she might have vanished to: "Blue Hawaii" and "The Moon of Manakoora" and "Twilight in Turkey." Every sad lyric seemed to have been written expressly for him, contrived to remind him of events that somehow never happened: "In the Still of the Night" and "I See Your Face Before Me," and especially "Where or When," which was all mystery and magic in the guise of *déjà vu*. He asked about her everywhere. "Long blond hair," he would say, "and brown eyes, and she was wearing a pale-blue dress and dust-covered sneakers. She's the most beautiful girl who ever lived." And he heard conflicting reports about her. Someone said Yes, he had seen her, she was visiting from California, staying with a cousin on South Twelfth—but he checked the address and the cousin did not exist. And someone else said he thought she worked for the carnival, a sort of shill—but the next time the carnival came to town, she was not with it. Hitler was about to march into Poland; the world was poised for war; but all he could think of was the girl with the long blond hair.

In the early part of 1942 the area of his search was enlarged. He went into the Navy, and the Navy took him to the Great Lakes Training Center and Chicago, and then to radar school in Fort Lauderdale, and the opportunity to search Miami and Miami Beach, and then Norfolk for a training course with the assembled crew of his about-to-be-commissioned ship. He went as far as Richmond looking for her, and then Boston to commission the destroyer, and Guantanamo for a shakedown cruise, and the Panama Canal and a quick, one-night search of Colón, and then San Diego, and Pearl Harbor, searching, always searching —and then the ship went into action, and he stopped looking because then there was nothing to see but death.

His best friend aboard ship was another radarman named Clyde Morrow. He often told him about the girl with no name, and he speculated for the first time about what might have happened if he hadn't said "Yes" to her request. Would she have vanished so completely if he hadn't agreed to stay there by the river? The idea was a nagging one. Discussing it with Clyde on the fantail of the *Fancher,* he recognized his acquiescence as a committed error. But he did not yet know it would become a trend, and then a habit, and eventually a trap. He was, after all, an enlisted man in the United States Navy, subject to commands, becoming more and more accustomed to saying, "Yes, sir." As the years passed, as the *Fancher* miraculously survived battle after battle, the mandatory "Yes, sir" became second nature to him, the ship became his home, his crewmates became the only community he knew. He had never had any brothers, and now Clyde Morrow, mild and unassuming, quietly understanding, became a brother to him. In November of 1948 he said "Yes" to his brother, and lost him, and became frightened.

The *Fancher* had got under way at dusk, part of a force escorting the four transports and two cargo vessels out of Ironbottom Sound on their way to Espíritu Santo to the southwest. The action itself, the very fact that the transports and cargo ships had been ordered away from Guadalcanal, was an ominous one. Even if there had not been the heavy Japanese air attack that afternoon, the men would have known instantly that something was in the wind. He was not surprised when the chemical alarm shrieked its warning through the ship a little after midnight. Automatically he swung his legs over the side of his bunk, pulled on his trousers, and slipped his feet into his shoes. He was putting on his chambray shirt and running for the ladder when Clyde called to him.

There was something curiously compelling in his voice. Turning, he looked into Clyde's eyes and saw something there he had never seen before.

"What is it?" he whispered.

Behind them, the speaker on the bulkhead blared, "General Quarters! All hands, man your battle stations! General Quarters!"

"What is it, Clyde?"

Sailors were rushing past them, scrambling up the single ladder leading out of the aft sleeping compartment, pulling on clothing as they ran.

"What is it, for God's sake?"

"I can't go up there again."

"What?"

"The bridge," Clyde said. "I can't." He shook his head. "Can't," he said again.

"What do you mean? Clyde, that's General Quarters. We've got to . . ."

"Listen."

"What?"

"Listen. I . . . I can't go up there." Clyde's fingers tightened on the pale-blue sleeve of his shirt. "I . . . I could see the pilot's face. This afternoon. When the . . . when the plane dove at the bridge, I could see his face. And . . . and flames were dropping from the fuselage . . . on . . . on . . . some dropped on my helmet." Clyde paused and swallowed. "I can't go up there again. I don't care. I can't go up."

"Well . . . well, what . . . ?" He looked around him in panic. The compartment was almost clear now. They stood together by the ladder, the chemical alarm still shrieking, Clyde's hand tight on his sleeve.

"Switch with me," Clyde said abruptly. "Take my place on the bridge."

"How can I do that?"

"The old man doesn't know what the hell's going on, anyway. He doesn't care who his talker is, so long as he's got one."

"Clyde, he'd—"

"I'll take your place at the Sugar George in the radar shack. You go up and handle the phones. Please."

"I can't do that, Clyde."

"Please."

"How can I . . . ?"

"I thought we were friends," Clyde said.

"Yes, but . . ."

"Then please! Can't you see I'm about to—"

"All right," he said softly. "Yes, Clyde. All right, I'll do it. But for God's sake, hurry!"

He would remember that night as long as he lived as a night of confusion and terror, Friday the thirteenth, a jinx of a night. There were fourteen American warships and only twelve Japanese. but the Japanese numbered two battlewagons in their force, and the early American advantage of radar was somehow lost in the baffled confusion of a voice radio circuit that was carrying radar reports from the *Fancher* together with commands on course, speed, and gunfire from the flagship . . . until suddenly the Japanese fleet loomed out of the darkness not a breath away, and then radar didn't matter a damn.

They came upon each other with shocking swiftness, meeting in the sound between Cape Esperance and Lunga Point, anticipating the contact and then suddenly surprised to find themselves in the middle of a desperate fight. Japanese searchlights blinked into the night, long fingers of illumination sweeping the water, capturing the surprised and frightened looks on the faces of American sailors as the orders to commence firing and counter-illuminate were roared by the gunnery officer. Standing on the bridge of the *Fancher* in Clyde's usual battle position, the sound-powered phones on his head, the mouthpiece an inch away from his lips, he relayed urgent radar reports to the exec and watched the world disintegrate in fire. The roar of the guns was deafening, salvo after salvo pouring from the batteries, sending shudder after shudder through the length of the ship. No one seemed to know exactly what was happening. Each ship that cruised by silently in the darkness could easily be the enemy. Searchlights winked on and off with frightening suddenness; tracer shells threaded the night like blinking neon, red and white; billows of thick black oil smoke belched up from the ships. The sea churned with the geyser-white spray of exploding shells; the night itself was a churning cacophony of fire and smoke and shouts.

Another searchlight pierced the blackness and caught the bridge of the *Fancher* in brilliant, merciless illumination. He heard the big Japanese guns bellowing in the blackness, heard the shells as they screamed across the open water, and then the *Fancher* rocked with explosion and he lost his footing as the deck swung downward to port, slanting under his feet. Someone on the open bridge yelled, "The radar shack! They hit Combat!" He tried to scramble to his feet. Crouching against the bulkhead of the pilothouse, the bridge slanting, the whole ship slanting —*I'll fall off*, he thought wildly, *I'll drown*—he pressed the button on his mouthpiece.

"Combat, this is Bridge," he said, and got no answer from the radar shack.

"Combat, Bridge!" he shouted urgently. "Was that a hit?" Silence, "Hey! Can anybody hear me? Clyde, are you on this line? Clyde? Clyde?" Silence. "Will you for Christ's sake answer?"

The action ended at about 0230, when the remaining Japanese warships began limping northward. The Americans had lost four destroyers and two light cruisers. Almost every ship in the force was badly damaged, but the planes on Henderson Field—the Japanese objective—

had been saved. The *Fancher,* floating on an oil-slicked sea adrift with white hats and the bodies of sailors hanging lifelessly inside their life jackets, extinguished her fires by 1930 and once more considered it a miracle that she was afloat. The tropical sun was brilliant on the warm Pacific waters. The sailors took off their shirts as they worked to clean up the mess.

The explosion in the radar shack had wounded the senior communications officer, destroyed the Sugar George gear, and killed a Radarman Second/Class named Clyde Morrow.

It was not his fault, and logically he knew it was not his fault. But logic and reason seemed to have no place in his reconstruction of what had happened. Piece by painful piece he put the incident together, and the resulting revelation was frightening. He hadn't wanted to go up to the bridge any more than Clyde had, but neither had he wanted to lose Clyde's friendship. And so he had taken the easy way out; he had chosen not to argue. He had said "Yes" and sent Clyde to his death. As frightening as the knowledge was, he persisted in exploring it and finally coupled it with what had happened by the river on the night of the carnival. He had said "Yes" there, too, and sent the girl into oblivion.

"Yes," then, was a dangerous word. Here in a world of snapping hand salutes and of mechanical responses to idiotic orders he began to dread the word and what it meant in terms of his own weakness. He resolved to be extremely careful with its use. He knew now that he was inclined to avoid friction, to present the agreeable smile and the accepting nod rather than to risk displeasure. But on at least two occasions he had gambled on a nod—and lost. He decided he would never allow that to happen again.

He was twenty-seven years old when he was released from active duty in 1946 and returned to his home town. He felt a lot older. The town had changed very little during the war, but it seemed alien and strange to him. He avoided making new friendships because friendship involved a responsibility he had decided against. He took a series of meaningless jobs, leaving one after another whenever he got bored or whenever he felt too much was being demanded of him. Without fully realizing it, he was becoming aimless and rootless, bound by a futile decision that really rendered him decisionless. He had, in effect, committed himself to a policy of non-commitment, and perhaps he realized it would not work even before he met Beth.

He supposed he would never love anyone as deeply as he had loved the girl with the blond hair. Beth had blond hair, too, but she wasn't that enchanting girl of his youthful dreams, not by any wild imagining. Beth's hair was clipped short, and her eyes were blue, and there was a somewhat horsy look to her face, a sophisticated twang to her speech. She walked over to him one night at a club dance and said, "My name is Beth McCauley. Don't you ever talk to anyone?"

"Sure I do," he said. "What do you want me to say?"

"I'd like you to ask me to dance."

"Do you want to dance?" he said.

"I'd love to," Beth answered, and she flashed a quick, conspiratorial grin.

She danced well. She was a small girl who seemed too compactly built, but she moved with surprising grace, and she followed every innuendo of pressure on the small of her back. He walked down to the river with her later. The waters were black; the willows overhung the bank. He thought he could hear a trace of laughter floating on the air.

"I used to come here when I was a kid," he told her.

"It's beautiful," she said.

"Mmmm." He nodded and looked at the water. He guessed he should kiss her.

"You haven't told me your name," she said suddenly.

The words startled him. He looked at her curiously and then very softly and slowly said, "My name is the wind."

"What?" Beth said, and then laughed. "It isn't at all. It's Matt. I knew before I asked you to dance." She paused. "What's your last name?"

"Blaney. Why?"

"Blaney," she repeated, and then suddenly added, "Beth Blaney," as if testing the words.

He made no comment. He shrugged in the darkness, and then he kissed her without any real desire and thought, *You can feel her teeth when you kiss her.*

There was passion in this girl, and beauty of a sort, and a knife-edge intelligence that sometimes made him feel awkward and clumsy. But most of the time she was pleasant and easy to be with, and he continued seeing her until eventually she seemed to have been there always.

He had no intention of marrying her, not really. Even facing the realization that he could not go through life refusing to form any real attachments, he did not once seriously think of forming an attachment with Beth Mc-Cauley. He continued seeing her because she demanded nothing of him. Until one night, by the river, suddenly and without preamble, she said, "Matt, I want to get married."

At first, idiotically, he thought she was talking about someone else. And then immediately he knew she meant she wanted to marry him, and the idea was so preposterous that he almost laughed aloud. *Well, I don't want to marry you,* he thought and said nothing, staring at the river.

"Well?" she said.

"Well, what do you want me to say?"

"Say yes or no, Matt."

Yes or no, he thought, and he smiled a bit wryly. Yes or no, and what happens if I say "Yes"? Who vanishes this time, Beth? Who gets blasted into oblivion?

"I haven't given much thought to marriage," he said cautiously.

"Think about it now, Matt."

I don't have to think about a damn thing, he thought. *I know I don't want to marry you. I don't love you. What's there to think about?*

"I can't afford to get married right now," he said. "I'm going to leave my job. I'm fed up with my job."

"My father will give you a job, Matt."

I don't want a job with your father, he thought. *I don't even like your father.*

"I don't know anything about grain," he said.

"You don't have to know a goddamn thing," she answered angrily, "and he'll still pay you twenty thousand a year."

"That's a lot of money."

"Yes."

"I'd hate to think I was being . . ."

"Bribed?" Beth supplied.

"Well . . ."

"You are," she said. "I'm twenty-eight years old, Matt, and I'm tired of necking by the river. Yes or no?"

"If I say no?"

"Is that your answer?" She rose and brushed off her skirt.

"Wait!"

"Yes or no, Matt?"

"How do you know I love you?" he said.

"I didn't ask," Beth answered.

He hesitated for a long while. Then, committing himself for the first time since Clyde's death, he said, "Yes, all right," and knew instantly who would vanish this time, knew instantly who would be blasted into oblivion.

They were married in the First Episcopal Church on top of the hill. Her family made all the arrangements, and he always looked back on it later as Beth's wedding, not his own. The house they moved into was chosen by Beth, a high-gabled house in the middle of a dense woods. Later, because the house was in the middle of the woods, Beth insisted that they buy a gun. Apparently she had already forgotten that she herself had chosen the house and its location. That didn't matter. She was afraid of being alone in the woods, she said, now that they had children to care for. By that time he was so used to saying "Yes" that he'd protested only weakly before agreeing and then went downtown with her to pick out the Savage. He hadn't liked the gun from the start. The gun reminded him of the .22 he'd been firing that night at the carnival when the enchanted girl—he always thought of her as enchanted, magical—had walked soundlessly into his life on silent, sneakered feet. The gun reminded him of the

five-inch cannons on the *Fancher* and the answering fire of
the Japanese ships, and the death of Clyde Morrow.

But more than that, the gun—securely locked in a rack,
out of reach of the children—was a constant and visible
reminder of what he had become, or perhaps what he had
always been. Yes, yes, yes, I will marry you, yes I like the
house with the gables in the middle of the woods, yes we
should have children, yes we need a gun, yes, yes!

This afternoon he had said "Yes" for the last time.

He picked up the shotgun he had not wanted and
thought, *You goddamn gun, I didn't want you!*

I didn't want Beth, *or* this endless silent house, *or* the
children, *or* the job with her father where Alan can come
in to ask me to do something meaningless and I can say,
"Yes, sure, fine, yes, yes!"

I would like to say "No" sometime, he thought. I would
like to stand with my head and shoulders back. I would
like to take a deep breath and then yell with all my
strength, "No! I don't want to, you bastards!"

He looked at the shotgun. He sighed gently and then
put the barrel into his mouth and hooked his thumb
around the trigger.

I don't want to do this, he thought.

And fired.

THE INNOCENT ONE

IT WAS PABLO, poor bastard, who got it.

You must understand, first, that the sun was very hot on that day and Miguel had been working in it from just after dawn. He had eaten a hearty breakfast and then had taken to the fields early, remembering what had to be done and wanting to do it quickly.

There were many stones among the beans that day, and perhaps that is what started it all. When Miguel discovered the first stone, he reached down gingerly and tossed it over his shoulder to the rear of his neat rows or beans. The sun was still not high in the sky, and the earth had not yet begun to bake, and so a smile worked its way over his brown features as he heard the stone thud to the soft earth behind him. He started hoeing again, thinking of Maria and the night before.

He would never regret having married her. Ah, but she was a one! There was the beauty of the lark in her, and the passion of the tigress, and the energy of the . . .

He saw the second stone.

He shrugged, thinking, *Madre de Dios, another one!*

He lifted it, threw it over his shoulder, and began hoeing again. He was surprised when he came across more stones. At first he thought someone had played a joke on him, and he pulled his black brows together, wondering who it could have been. Juan, that pig? Felipe, that animal with the slobbering lips? Pablo?

Then he remembered that it had rained the night before. and he realized that the waters had washed the soil clean. exposing the stones, bringing them to the surface.

He cursed himself for not having thought to protect the beans in some way. Then he cursed the stones. And since the sun was beginning to climb in the sky, he cursed that, too, and got to work.

The stones were not heavy. They were, in fact, rather small.

It was that there were very many of them. He picked them up painstakingly, tossing them over his shoulders. How could a man hoe his beans when the rows were full of stones? He started to count them, stopping at ten because that was as far as he knew how to count, and then starting with one all over again.

The sun was very hot now. The hoe lay on the ground, the rich earth staining its long handle. He kept picking up the stones, not looking up now, swearing softly, the sweat pouring down his neck and back. A long shadow fell over the land before him, and then a voice joined the shadow, and Miguel straightened his back and rubbed his earth-stained fingers on his white trousers.

"You are busy, Miguel?" the voice asked. The voice came through the speaker's thick lips. It bubbled like the voice of the kettle. It was Felipe.

"No, I am not busy," Miguel said. "I was, at this very moment, lying on my back and counting the stars in the sky."

"But it is only morn—" Felipe started. Miguel's subtle humor struck him then, and he slapped his thigh and commenced to guffaw like the jackass he was. "Counting the stars!" he bellowed. "Counting the stars!"

Miguel was not amused. "You were perhaps on your way somewhere, *amigo*. If so, do not let me detain you."

"I was going nowhere, Miguel," Felipe said.

Miguel grunted and began picking up stones again. He

forgot how many tens he had counted thus far, so he started all over again.

"You are picking up stones, Miguel?"

Miguel did not answer.

"I say you are picking up—"

"Yes!" Miguel said. "Yes, I am picking up stones." He stood up and kneaded the small of his back, and Felipe grinned knowingly.

"The back, it hurts, eh?"

"Yes," Miguel said. He looked at Felipe. "Why do you nod?"

"Me? Nod? Who, me?"

"Yes, you. Why do you stand there and nod your head like the wise snake who has swallowed the young chicken?"

Felipe grinned and nodded his head. "You must be mistaken, Miguel. I do not nod."

"I am not blind, *amigo*," Miguel said testily. "I say my back hurts, and you begin to nod your head. Why? Is it funny that my back hurts? Is it funny that there are stones among my beans?"

"No, Miguel. It is not funny."

"Then why do you nod?"

Felipe grinned. "Maria, eh?"

Miguel clenched his fists. "What about Maria, who is my wife?"

Felipe opened his eyes innocently. "Nothing, Miguel, nothing. Just . . ." He shrugged. "Maria."

"You refer to my back?"

"*Si.*"

"And you connect this somehow with Maria?"

"*Si.*"

"How?"

"This Maria—your wife, God bless her—she is a strong one, eh, Miguel?"

Miguel was beginning to get a little angry. He was not used to discussing his wife among the beans. "So? What do you mean she is a . . . a strong one?"

"You know. Much passion. Like the tigress."

"How do you know this?"

Felipe grinned. "I do not know it, Miguel."

Miguel's lips tightened into a narrow line. "Then if you do not know it, how is it that you know it?"

"I must go to town, Miguel," Felipe said hastily. "I will see you soon."

"Just a moment, Felipe. How is it—"

"Goodbye, *amigo.*"

Felipe turned his back, and Miguel stared at him as he walked toward the road. The dust rose about him, and he waved back at Miguel. Miguel did not return the wave. He stood there with the strong sun on his head and the many stones at his feet.

How did this animal with the slobbering lips know of Maria's passion? Surely he had never spoken a word about it to any of the men. Then how did Felipe know?

The possibilities annoyed Miguel. He turned back to the stones, and this time they seemed heavier, and the sun seemed stronger, and his back seemed to ache more.

How did Felipe know?

He was pondering this in an ill temper when Juan came to stand beside him. Juan was darkly handsome, his white trousers and shirt bright in the powerful sunlight. Miguel looked up at him sourly and said, "So? Do you wish to pass the time with idle chatter also?"

Juan smiled, his teeth even and white against the ruddy brown of his face. "Did I offend you, Miguel?"

"No!" Miguel snapped.

"Then why do you leap at me like a tiger?"

"Do not mention this animal to me," Miguel said.

"No?"

"No! I have stones to clear, and I want to clear them before lunch because Maria will be calling me then."

"Ahhh," Juan said, grinning.

Miguel stared at him for a moment. The grin was the same one Felipe had worn, except that Felipe was ugly and with slobbering lips—and Juan was perhaps the handsomest man in the village.

Miguel stared at him and wondered if it had been *he* who had told Felipe of Maria's great passion. And if so, how had Juan known?

"Why do you 'ahhhhh'" he asked.

"Did I 'ahhhhh'?"

"You did. You did indeed. You made this very sound. Why?"

"I was not aware, *amigo.*" Juan smiled again.

"Was it mention of lunch that evoked this sigh?"

"No. No, I do not think so."

"Then there remains only Maria."

Juan grinned and said nothing.

"I said—"

"I heard you, Miguel."

"What about Maria?"

Juan shrugged. "Who said anything about Maria?"

"You are saying it with your eyes," Miguel said heatedly. "What about her?"

"She is your wife, Miguel."

"I know she is my wife."

Juan was grinning again.

"What is so funny about that? Why do you grin now?"

"I have nothing to say, *amigo*. Maria is your wife. God bless her."

"What does that mean?"

"It means . . . well, God bless her. She is a remarkable woman."

"How would you know?" Miguel shouted.

"That she is a remarkable woman? Why, Miguel . . ."

"You know what I mean! What is going on? Why do you all discuss my wife so intimately? What—"

"Intimately?"

"Yes! Juan, if there is something . . ."

Juan smiled again. "But there is nothing, Miguel. Nothing."

"You are sure?"

"I must go to town now, my friend. Is there anything I can do for you there?"

"No!" Miguel snapped.

"Then, *adiós, amigo*."

He turned and walked off, shaking his head, and Miguel could have sworn he heard him mutter the word "tigress."

He went to work on the stones with a fury. What was all this? Why Felipe? And now Juan?

What was going on with his wife?

He thought of her passion, her gleaming black hair, the way it trailed down the curve of her back, reaching her waist. He thought of the fluid muscles on that back beneath the soft, firm skin. He thought of the long, graceful sweep of her legs, the way the firelight played on her lifted breasts.

Too passionate, he thought.

Far too passionate for simple Miguel who worked in the fields picking stones and hoeing beans. Perhaps she was a woman who needed more than one man, yes, who needed many men, yes, who needed many, many, many men.

Was that why Felipe had laughed with his dripping lips? Was that why Juan had smiled that superior, handsome smile? Miguel picked up his hoe and swung it at a large rock. The rock chipped, but it did not budge from the earth.

Was that it? Was Maria making a cuckold of her simple Miguel? Was that why all the men in the village were snickering, smiling, laughing behind their hands? Or was it only the men from this village? Was it the adjoining village as well? Or did it go beyond that? To the next town? To the nearest city? To all Mexico?

Did they pass her from hand to hand like a used wine jug? Did they all drink of her, and was that why they laughed at Miguel now? Was that why they laughed behind their hands, laughed aloud with their mouths and their eyes?

The sun was hot, and the bowels of the earth stank, and the rock would not be budged from the ground. Miguel chopped at it with the hoe, using the sharp blade like an ax.

I will show them, he thought. I will teach them to laugh! I will teach them to put the horns on Miguel de la Piaz!

It was then that Pablo strolled by. He had passed Miguel's house, and Maria had asked him to call her husband home for lunch. He was not a bright person, Pablo. He walked up close to Miguel, who furiously pounded the earth with his hoe, using it like an ax, the sharp blade striking sparks from the rock. He tapped Miguel on the shoulder, smiled, and started to say, "Maria . . ."

Miguel whirled like an animal, the hoe raised high.

So you see, it was Pablo, poor bastard, who got it

PRETTY EYES

S HE WAS THIRTY-THREE years old.

She was not a pretty woman, and she knew it.

The bellhop who showed her to the room in the Miami Beach hotel whistled all the way up in the elevator, whistled as he unlocked the door and stepped aside for her to enter.

"Nice room," he said. "Best on the floor. Has a balcony overlooking the ocean. Get the cool sea breezes." He grinned. He was no more than nineteen, a red-headed boy with a leering wisdom far beyond his years. "First time in Miami?" he asked.

"No."

"Been here before?"

"Yes," she said. "I come down every year."

"Oh?" The bellhop was still grinning. "First time at this hotel?"

"Yes."

"It's a good hotel." He put the valises on the stand. "You're not married, are you?"

"No," she answered, "I'm not married."

"Must get lonely, a pretty girl travelling all alone."

She looked at his face, and saw the lie sitting in his eyes. She said nothing.

"If you get ... uh ... *too* lonely," the bellhop said, his grin widening, "why, just buzz the desk. My name's Johnny. Be happy to ... uh ... come up and chat or something."

"Thank you," she said. There were four valises. She had read somewhere that a bellhop's services were worth twenty-five cents per bag. She never tipped more than twenty-five cents per bag and never less. She took a dollar from her purse and handed it to him.

"Thanks," he said briskly, lifting his coat and stuffing the bill into his watch pocket. "Anything I can get you?"

"No, thank you."

"If you hurry, you can still catch a swim and some sun."

"Thank you," she said.

At the door he repeated, "My name's Johnny," and then he left. Alone in the room, she began unpacking. Every year it was like this. The drive to the airport alone. The flight down alone. The cab ride to the hotel—a different one each year—alone. The unpacking. Alone.

A pretty girl travelling all alone.

His lie still rankled. She was not a pretty girl. She had discovered this a long time ago. The discovery had been painful, but she'd adjusted to it. She was not pretty. Her hair was a lusterless brown, and her eyes were a faded gray, and her nose was too long, and her mouth was too thin and her figure was put together awkwardly. She was not pretty. Nor, she supposed, was she any longer a girl. Thirty-three. And next year thirty-four. And then thirty-five. And forty.

And alone.

The room was silent except for the steady hum of the air conditioner. She unpacked her bags and then went out onto the balcony. She could see the azure of the pool nine stories below, the men and women lounging around it in deck chairs. A muted sound of voices hung over the pool area, washed by the steady roll of the ocean against the beach beyond. She could almost see the bright golden shimmer of heat on the air, could taste the wet ocean salt on her mouth.

She wondered if it would happen this time.

The bellhop suddenly seemed an ill omen. His intentions had been clear, absolutely clear. Nor would he have so obviously spoken his mind had she been a pretty woman. A pretty woman somehow generated fear and respect. A plain woman did not. A plain woman was a lonely woman, and men sensed this. Oh, not lonely for the night, no. It was never difficult to find a transitory partner for the night. She had found many such partners, ever since the first time when she'd been twenty-six—she could still remember it clearly, remember the desolation she had felt, the sudden feeling that life was slipping away too fast and that she would die a dried-up old maid. And since that time there had been many, and she knew the approaches now, the pat approaches, the bold, bald propositions: "What's a pretty girl like you doing all alone on a night like this?" "Why don't we have a drink in my room?" "Come on, beautiful, what do you have to lose?" She knew them all; she had heard them all.

But this time it will be different, she vowed. *This time it has to be different.*

Purposefully she changed to her swimsuit and took the elevator down to the pool.

Sitting alone at the bar that night, she could feel her skin tingling, and she wondered if she'd taken too much sun that afternoon. Luckily she did not turn lobster red the way some girls did. She tanned steadily and graciously, and there had been a time when she'd thought she was more attractive with a tan, but she no longer believed this. Still, she was thankful that she tanned rather than burned, and she wondered now if she had taken too much sun, wondered if she would spend a sleepless night.

She reached into her purse for a cigarette, put it between her lips, and was digging into her purse for matches when the lighter sprang into flame at the cigarette's end.

"Allow me," the man said.

She turned slightly on the stool. "Thank you," she said in cool aloofness, raising one eyebrow. She sucked at the flame and then blew out a cloud of smoke and turned away from the man, back to her whiskey sour.

The man sat on the stool next to hers. He was silent for a moment and then he said, "Do you like those filter tips?"

"What?"

"The cigarette."

"Oh. Yes, I do."

"I never feel I'm smoking with a filter tip," the man said.

"I don't mind them," she answered. "It's a cleaner smoke, I feel."

"I suppose so," the man said. He ordered Scotch on the rocks from the bartender and then turned to her again. "Just check in?" he asked.

"This afternoon," she said.

"First time in Miami?"

"No, no," she said, smiling. "I've been here before."

"Are you with your husband, or is this just a rest?"

"I'm not married," she said.

"No?" he said. He smiled pleasantly. "My name's Jack Bryant," he said, extending his hand.

"Connie Davidson," she told him, and she took his hand. His grip was firm and warm. He released her hand almost instantly.

"Treating yourself to a vacation, is that it?" he asked.

"I come down here every year at this time," she said.

"Where are you from?"

"New York," she answered.

"What part?"

"Are you from New York, too?"

"Yes," he said. "Brooklyn."

"I'm from Manhattan," she said. "Shall I make the Brooklyn jokes?"

He grinned easily. His eyes crinkled at the corners when he grinned. He was a pleasant-looking man in his late thirties, with warm blue eyes set in a tanned, even face. "I'd rather you didn't," he said. "I'm a criminal lawyer. I defend most of the people the jokes are about."

"That must be fascinating work," she said.

"It is. It gets a little tiring, though."

"Are you here on business?" she asked.

"No, no. Just a rest." He sipped at his Scotch. "What sort of work do you do?"

"I work for an advertising agency."

"Doing what?"

"I write jingles."

"Really? No! You mean Pepsi-Cola? Like that?"

"Well, not Pepsi-Cola. But like that."

"Well, that's wonderful. You know, you hear the jingles, but you never realize somebody wrote them. It must be fun."

"It is," she said, smiling. "But it can get tiring, too."

He looked at her empty glass. "Would you like another drink?"

"Thank you," she said. "I would."

He ordered for her. They sat silently for a while, and then he said, "Here comes the band. Would you like to dance?"

"Not right now," she said.

"You look like a good dancer."

"I'm fair," she said.

"I'll bet you've taken lessons."

"What makes you say that?"

"I don't know. I just get that feeling."

"I took a few. For the mambo."

"And the cha-cha?"

"No. I stopped before that became the rage."

"There's always a new one," he said, chuckling. "After the cha-cha it'll be the ha-ha or the ho-ho. I think if you know the fox trot, the rhumba, and the waltz, that's all you have to know. Unless you're a fanatic for dancing."

"Well, I like to dance," she said.

"Oh, I do, too. But you can't make it your life's work."

"No, I suppose not."

"How long will you be staying, Connie?" he asked.

"Two weeks."

"Isn't that a coincidence?" he said.

"You'll be here . . ."

"Another two weeks, yes." He paused. "We can have a lot of fun together."

"Well," she said.

"I always wonder how it feels," he said.

"What?"

"You know."

"No, what?"

"A pretty girl like you," he said, "traveling alone."

She looked at him steadily.

"It . . . it feels fine," she answered.

"Must get lonely."

"Not too," she answered.

"Well, it seems to me it must get lonely," he said.

"I . . . I don't mind it," she said.

"Well, we'll have fun," he said, and he covered her

hand with his. She did not move her hand for several moments. Then she slid it from his and picked up her drink.

"Think you could teach me the mambo?" he asked.

"Anyone can learn it," she answered.

"It seems so difficult."

"No."

"It seems that way," he said. "I'm always afraid I'll make a fool of myself on the dance floor."

"It's really very simple."

"Just a matter of getting the rhythm, I suppose," he said. "Still, with all those experts on the floor . . ." He shook his head ruefully, embarrassedly.

She knew what was coming next. She could have said the words even before they left his mouth. For a moment she wished desperately that she were wrong, wished that he would not say what she was sure he would say. For a moment she wished that once—just once—a man would look at her and honestly believe she had beautiful hair, or a fine brow, or pretty eyes. Once, just once, and her heart would open like a flower and the warmth would pour from her, the warmth that was stored, ready to burst. Just once, just once . . .

And then he said, "Maybe you could give me private lessons."

She did not answer.

"It's a little stuffy in here anyway, isn't it?" he asked.

"A . . . a little," she said.

"The air conditioner in my room works fine," he said. He smiled pleasantly.

"I . . . I don't know," she answered.

"We could order some drinks up there," he said. "I'd be honored. A pretty girl like you teaching me how to dance. I'd be honored."

"Please," she said.

"Seriously. We could dance a little . . ."

"Please . . ."

". . . and drink a little . . ."

"Please, please . . ."

"You know, have a little fun," he concluded.

She looked at his face soberly. The lie was in his eyes and on his mouth. Blankly she said, "I'm not pretty."

"Sure you are," he answered. "You're one of the prettiest girls in the hotel."

She nodded briefly. Her eyes dropped to the bar. She could see his left hand and the narrow band of white flesh on his third finger, where a ring had belatedly been removed after the skin had tanned.

"You're married?" she asked.

"Yes."

She nodded silently.

"Does it matter?" he asked.

"No," she said. "It doesn't matter. Nothing matters." She rose. "Good night," she said. "Thanks for the drink."

"Hey, what about the private lessons?"

She did not answer. Her eyes were misting as she walked away from the bar.

She checked out that night.

There did not seem to be any sense in staying. There did not seem to be any sense in anything. She wore a white linen suit, and she stood in the hotel corridor with the bellhop, impatiently waiting for the elevator, anxious to get away.

The elevator door slid open. She entered the car, and the bellhop followed with her four valises. A man was standing in one corner of the elevator. He looked at her

when she entered. The car dropped leisurely toward the
lobby. The man seemed rather nervous, a man of about
thirty-five, with solemn brown eyes. He seemed as if he
wanted to speak to her, but instead he swallowed
repeatedly until the elevator had almost reached the
lobby floor.

And then, at last, he very quietly said, "You have pretty
eyes. The—" He glanced self-consciously at the bellhop
and the elevator operator. "—the prettiest eyes I've ever
seen."

She turned to him, naked hatred gleaming on her face.
Sharply she whispered, "Stop it! Damn you, damn you,
stop it!"

The elevator door slid open.

"Lobby," the operator said.

She stepped out of the car. The man looked at the
operator in embarrassment. He waited for the bellhop to
leave the car, and then he stepped into the lobby. He
watched while she settled her bill. He watched while the
bellhop carried her bags out and hailed a cab. He watched
as the cab pulled away from the hotel, the girl sitting
alone on the back seat. The bellhop returned to the
lobby, pocketing a dollar bill.

"Touchy broad, huh?" he said to the man.

The man did not answer for a long while. He kept
staring through the wide plate-glass doors at the empty
street outside where the girl in the cab had been.

Then he said, "She had pretty eyes. She had very
pretty eyes."

He bought a newspaper at the cigar stand in the arcade
and sat in the lobby, reading, until midnight.

Alone in his silent room, he went to bed.

MILLION DOLLAR MAYBE

JOHN WAS SHOWING me the illustrations for the June issue when the buzzer on my desk sounded.

"This fellow is terrific," he said. "I mean it, Bert, we're lucky we got him at all—and especially at the price we're paying."

"I still think it's too high," I said. I reached over and snapped down the toggle. "Yes?"

"Mr. Merrian?"

"Yes?"

"There's a gentleman here to see you, sir."

"Who?" I asked.

"A Mr. Donald, sir."

"*Who?*"

"Mr. Donald."

"I don't know any Mr. Donald." I turned to John. "You know any Mr. Donald?" He shook his head, and I turned my face back to the speaker. "Ask him what it's in reference to, will you?"

"Yes, sir."

With my forefinger I tapped the illustration John was holding. "We start paying these people fancy prices, and we'll put ourselves out of business."

"Fancy?" John protested. "This is half what he gets from the better magazines. The only reason he did it for us is because I knew him in college."

"You can't trust artists," I told him. "Next thing you know, he'll be spreading the good news around. We'll have a steady stream of characters with portfolios under their arms. And you now how often we can afford five hundred."

"All right, so this is an exception."

"Damn right it is. You got the good drawing you were crying for, but I expect it to last you for the next five years."

"Mr. Merrian?" a female voice interrupted.

"Yes, I'm still here."

"Mr. Donald said he would like his million dollars."

"Hello?" I said.

"Yes, sir?"

"What did you just say?"

"I said Mr. Donald would like his million dollars."

"You see, John?" I said. "It's started already. I told you you can't trust artists. Well, I'll put a stop to this foolishness right away." I turned back to the intercom. "Send Mr. Donald in. And tell him to leave his portfolio outside."

"He has no portfolio, sir."

"Send him in anyway." I snapped off the toggle angrily and glared at John. John shrugged, moving his shoulders in a gesture that said, "I'm only the art director here."

I leaned back in my chair and waited for the door to open. When it did, a tall, thin man stepped into the room, blinking his eyes against the sunlight that streamed through the blinds. He shielded his eyes with one hand and took three cautious steps toward the desk.

"Mr. Donald?" I asked.

"Yes, sir," he said hesitantly.

"How do you do, sir? I'm Bert Merrian, publisher of *Prince*, and this is John Hastings, my art director. Have a seat, won't you, sir?"

"Well, thank you. That's awfully nice of you . . . considering."

I watched him cross the room and settle himself in the

chair beside my desk. He had black shaggy eyebrows that all but covered pale, almost violet, eyes. He kept his brows pulled low, so that his eyes showed only occasionally, like dim bulbs behind a darkroom curtain. His nose was thin, slicing down the center of his angular face like a machete slash. His lips were pressed firmly together. He looked like a man with unpleasant business on his mind. He certainly did not look like an artist.

"Well," I said cheerily, "what can we do for you, Mr. Donald?" I was beginning to enjoy this. I felt a little like an executioner putting his basket under the blade of the guillotine.

Mr. Donald smiled briefly, almost bashfully. "I'd like my million dollars," he said.

"Wouldn't we all?" I answered, chuckling a little.

His brows lifted slightly, and there was surprise in his pale eyes. "I guess we would at that," he said. He chuckled, too, and John joined in, and we had a short round of laughs until I coughed abruptly and called it to a halt.

"How did you . . . ah . . . intend getting your million dollars?" I asked, a pleasant smile on my face.

The brows went up again. "Why, from *Prince*."

"From *Prince*," I repeated. I turned to my art director and said meaningfully, "From *Prince*, John."

"Yes," Mr. Donald said.

"Yes," I repeated. "And just exactly what for? Would you mind telling us?"

"Not at all," Mr. Donald said, making himself comfortable in his chair. "For the moon trip, of course."

"The . . . what?"

Mr. Donald pointed up toward the ceiling with his extended forefinger. "The moon trip. You know."

"The *moon* trip? You mean moon? M-o-o-n? Our satellite? The moon?"

"Uh-huh," Mr. Donald said, nodding his head.

I leaned over toward John and whispered, "Did we run a piece about the moon lately?" John shook his head. "What the hell is this bird talking about?" John shook his head again. I sighed and turned back to Mr. Donald.

"Just exactly what did you have in mind about the moon trip?" I asked, pretending to know what it was all about.

Mr. Donald shrugged bashfully. "Well . . . I been."

"You been? What do you mean?"

Mr. Donald pointed up at the ceiling again. "The moon. I been."

"Oh-oh," I said.

"Yep," Mr. Donald agreed, nodding.

I looked quickly at John, and he returned my anxious glance. We were both beginning to realize that Mr. Donald was perhaps a little bit removed from his perch on the rocker.

He shrugged again. "So," he said casually, "I just come for the million dollars. If you'll let me have it, I'll be on my way."

"You figure we owe you a million dollars, is that it?"

"Oh, sure," Mr. Donald said.

"Uh . . . why? I mean . . ."

"Guess maybe it was a little before your time," Mr. Donald said. He fished into his wallet and came up with a folded sheet of paper. The paper was glossy, and there was printing on it. I watched him as he placed it on the desk and began unfolding it, portion by portion, section by section. He spread it all out, smoothed it with a browned hand, and then leaned back. "There," he said.

I looked at the sheet of paper, noticing that a rectangular portion had been cut from the bottom of it. I shrugged and shifted my eyes to the top of the sheet.

PRINCE Magazine . . . September, 1926

"Cut it out when the contest was announced," Mr. Donald said.

I looked at the page again. September 1926. Hell, that was almost forty years ago. I shifted my eyes and studied the page.

ATTENTION — IMPORTANT
ATTENTION — IMPORTANT
ATTENTION

Now that you have read the preceding article, *So You Think You'll Reach the Moon*, the publishers of *Prince* Magazine are ready to make a startling, unprecedented offer.

I heard a sudden gasp behind me, and I realized that John was reading over my shoulder and coming to the same horrible conclusion I myself was reaching. With morbid fascination I turned back to the frayed page from an ancient copy of our magazine.

Prince is ready to back up its conclusions with an offer of cold cash! We will pay *ONE MILLION DOLLARS* ($1,000,000), *ONE MILLION DOLLARS* to the first private citizen who reaches the moon and returns alive.

I was beginning to feel a little ill. I clutched the top of my desk and forced myself to read the rest of the page. Mr. Donald watched, a happy grin on his face.

> The rules of the contest are simple:
>
> 1—All contestants must be citizens of the United States of America.
> 2—The Moon Trip must be made within the next fifty years
> 3—The coupon at the bottom of this page must be mailed to *Prince* on or before October 15, 1926.
> 4—Employees or relatives of employees of any government agency are not eligible for entry in this . . .

"I ain't," Mr. Donald said.

"A relative, you mean," I said weakly.

"Or an employee."

"I didn't think you were."

Mr. Donald stretched leisurely. "Well, can I have the million dollars now?"

"Well . . . uh . . ." I looked hopefully to John.

"These things take a little time," John said quickly.

"Yes, yes, of course," I added. "A little time."

"Mmmm," Mr. Donald said.

"We . . . we have to check to see that your coupon is on file here," John said.

"Of course," I put in.

"It's on file," Mr. Donald said. He fished for his wallet again and came up with a small card. I winced and picked it up from the desk top. It read:

This is to certify that

~~Miss~~
~~Mrs.~~
Mr. _AMOS DONALD_____ has on this _23ʳᵈ_
day of _SEPTEMBER_____ ,1926, entered
into the *Prince* Magazine Moon Trip Contest.

~~Miss~~
~~Mrs.~~
It is understood that if Mr. _AMOS DONALD___
is the first private citizen to reach the moon and return

                                                her
alive, *Prince* Magazine will pay to him the sum of
one million dollars ($1,000,000) in United States
Currency. *J. Geoffrey Trimble*
                                    Publisher
                                    Prince Magazine

"We would need proof, of course," I said triumphantly, shoving the card across the desk.

"I got proof."

"Well, you bring it in," John said shrewdly. "We'll see about the million dollars then."

"Sure," Mr. Donald said, rising. "I'll have it tomorrow."

"We're closed tomorrow," I almost shouted.

"Monday, then. Ain't no rush."

"No rush at all," I agreed unenthusiastically.

Mr. Donald started for the door and opened it quickly.

"See you, fellas," he called, waving happily.

He stepped out of the room, and the door shut behind him. I reached quickly for the buzzer on my desk.

"Yes, sir?"

"Miss Davis, I want the September 1926 issue of *Prince* immediately!"

"Sir?"

"Can't you understand English? The September—"

"Yes, sir. Right away, sir."

I snapped off and turned quickly to John. He was pacing the floor anxiously, wringing his hands.

"I've heard stories about J.G.," I said. "They say he was a crazy bastard. They say he did anything to sell magazines."

"He couldn't have been *this* crazy," John moaned.

"No, no," I agreed. "A million dollars. Oh God, don't let it be true."

"I think it is," John wailed. "I think it's true."

The door opened, and Miss Davis fairly fell into the room, a strand of blond hair hanging over one eye. "I have it, sir," she beamed.

She held up a small container, and I started to say, "What the hell is—"

"Microfilm!" she announced.

"Give it here," I snapped. She handed me the container, and then left the office. John leaped to the wall cabinet, sliding it open and pulling out a portable viewer. He put the viewer on my desk, and I inserted the first strip, peering into the view plate. It was the cover of the old *Prince*. It showed a man with a bare chest, wrestling with an equally nude alligator. Splashed across the top of the magazine in bold red letters was the legend: PRINCE OFFERS $1,000,000 FOR FIRST MAN ON MOON!

"It's true," John wailed.

"I knew it. I knew it."

"Shall we read the article?"

"What for? It's true, John. We're ruined."

"There must be a loophole."

"Let's check that page again." I scanned through the strips until I came to the contest-offer page. I removed that from the pile and slipped it into the viewer. It was identical with the one Mr. Donald had shown us.

"There must be a loophole," John repeated.

"How? Where?"

John narrowed his eyes shrewdly. "There's always a loophole."

I clicked the toggle on the intercom.

"Yes, sir?"

"Get Stein, my lawyer. Tell him to get down here immediately. And check through our files. See if there's anyone still with the firm who was working for J. G. Trimble back in 1926."

"1926, sir?"

"My dear young lady, must I repeat everything to you six times?"

"1926, sir. Yes, sir."

She clicked off, only to come back on again in a few minutes.

"I have Mr. Stein for you, sir."

"I don't want him. Just tell him to get down here right away."

"Yes, sir."

"What are we going to do?" John asked.

"I don't know. Do you suppose this crazy old coot really went to the moon?"

"Impossible," John said firmly. "I'd bet a million dollars no one—"

"Please! Please."

"Sorry," John murmured.

The buzzer sounded, and I clicked on. "Yes?"

"There's a man working here, sir."

"Fine," I said. "Tell him to keep up the splendid—"

"I mean, he's been working here since 1926."

"Oh. Good, what's his name?"

"Malther. Ephraim Malther."

"What department is he in?"

"Shipping."

"How old is he?"

"Ninety-four, sir. He was ready for retirement years ago, but he elected to stay on."

"And he's in the shipping room?"

"Yes, sir. He's been there since 1926."

"Send him in," I said. "On the double."

"Yes, sir."

The shipping room was right downstairs, and I couldn't understand what took Ephraim Malther so long to climb the flight, especially when I'd specified "on the double." Until I saw him, of course. The door opened suddenly, and he stood there uncertainly, like a fragile leaf on an autumn tree. I glanced anxiously at the air circulator, and John quickly stabbed his thumb at the "Stop" button, just as the big vent threatened to suck the old man into its maw.

"Mr. Malther?" I asked.

"Yes, sir, Mr. Trimble, sir."

"I'm not Mr. Trimble," I told him. "I'm Mr. Merrian, the new publisher."

"Eh? Would you mind speaking a little louder, Mr. Trimble?"

The old man hobbled closer to the desk.

"I'm not Mr. Trimble," I shouted.

"How's that again?" he asked, cocking his head to one side. He had startlingly black hair, and rheumy blue eyes, and an annoying habit of lifting one brow high on his forehead when he spoke.

"Never mind," I bellowed. "What do you know about the moon trip?"

"Good idea, J.G.," he said. "I thought so in the beginning, and I still think so. One million dollars. Great publicity stunt."

"How is the firm protected?" I said. "How did they expect to raise a million dollars if anyone took them up on it?"

"Took them up on what?"

"The moon trip."

"Took *who* up?"

"Us. Took us up."

"To the moon? Shucks, Mr. Trimble, ain't no one gonna reach the moon. Heck, I'll bet a million doll—"

"Never mind," I shouted. "How is the company protected?"

"Fine," he said.

"Fine what? What on earth are you talking about?"

"The company's Detectives. Fine group of magazines. Should do well, Mr. Trimble."

"Oh, for Pete's sake."

"How's that?" He cocked his head to one side again.

"Look, try to understand. Some idiot claims he's reached the moon. He wants his million dollars. How are we going to pay it to him?"

Ephraim Malther spread his hands wide. "Shucks, Mr. Trimble, the insurance company will take care of that. Ain't nothing to worry about there."

"Of course!" John yelped.

I snapped my fingers and then clasped Malther to my bosom. "Naturally! Old J.G. would never have taken the

risk himself. An insurance company! Of course, of course."
I released Malther, and he almost fell to the floor. He
gathered himself together and I pointed my forefinger at
his chest.

"Which one?"

"Which one what, sir?"

"Which insurance company?"

"Oh. Lessee now."

"Think," I prompted.

"Think hard," John added.

Malther clapped his hands together. "Derrick and
Derrickson. That's who!"

"Thank God," I murmured. "You may go now, Mr.
Malther."

"Sir?"

"I said you may go now."

"Eh?"

I stepped around the desk and took Malther by the
elbow. "Go," I said. "Go. Back to the shipping room. Go.
Out. Goodbye." I steered him to the door, and then I
passed him outside.

"Thank you, Mr. Trimble," he said.

"Not at all."

"Eh?"

I turned back into the room, and the door shut on his
puzzled face. John was already thumbing through the
phone directory.

"Here it is," he said. "Derrick and Derrickson, twenty-
three branch offices."

"Where's the nearest one?"

"Fifth Avenue, corner of Thirty-eighth."

"Get on the phone, John. Make an appointment. I'm on
my way down now."

"Right!" he snapped.

I went to the door and opened it. I turned and looked at John solemnly, and he raised his arm.

"Godspeed, Bert!"

"Amen," I muttered.

The door shut behind me.

Peter Derrickson was an impressive-looking man in a conservative blue suit. His hair was snow white, and he sported a mustache of the same color under his somewhat bulbous nose.

His pretty redheaded secretary ushered me into his spacious office, and he motioned me to a chair near his desk.

"Your art director sounded upset," he said in a booming voice, as if he were shouting over a nationwide hookup.

I winced and said, "Well, he's excitable." I had decided on the way over that I was going to play this one cagily. I watched him now while he pounced on a fat cigar in a box on his desk. He put it between his teeth, chewed off one end, turned, and unceremoniously spit it past my ear. I heard the bitten-off end whistle by, and I opened my eyes wide in astonishment. Peter Derrickson didn't seem to notice my amazement.

"So," he boomed, "what's your problem, sir?"

"When J. G. Trimble was publisher of *Prince* Magazine, he took out a policy with your firm," I said.

Derrickson lit his cigar, and clouds of smoke billowed up around his head as he puffed heartily. A stream of smoke found the match, extinguished it. From behind the cloudy layers his voice boomed, "Lots of people take out policies with our firm."

"This one was for a million dollars."

Derrickson puffed some more, and I tried vainly to see him through the smoke screen.

"Lots of people take out million-dollar policies," a voice said from behind the billowing cloud.

"This one was insurance against a trip to the moon."

A white head popped out of the cloud. "Oh, *that* damn fool thing."

"Yes," I said.

"I remember," Derrickson shouted in his normal voice. "What about it?" His head retreated into the cloud once more, and I was once again talking to a shifting screen of smoke.

"That's what I wanted to ask you. What about it?"

"That's a good question," Derrickson roared. "I think the policy has lapsed."

"Lapsed?" I inquired weakly.

"Yes, lapsed," Derrickson bellowed. "I can remember when Trimble came to me with the idea. 'Hell, sure,' I said. 'Isn't any private citizen going to reach the moon in our time, Mr. Trimble. Oh, sure, maybe the military or some special agency, but a private citizen? Never. I'll give you a million-dollar policy, and I'll consider it a safe risk.' That's what I told him."

"And . . . and the policy has lapsed?"

"Yes, I believe so. Fact, I'm sure of it. Trimble stopped paying the premiums. Don't know why. They were ridiculously low."

"H—h—how low?"

"I just told you," Derrickson shouted. "*Ridiculously* low. You deaf or something, young man?"

"Why, no. I . . . I was just wondering how long ago the policy lapsed."

"I'd say about seven years ago. Why?"

"I just wondered. Would . . . would it be possible to pay up the back premiums and put the policy into effect again?"

"I don't know. Why? You worried someone's going to reach the moon before the government or the Russians?" For some strange reason Derrickson thought this was funny. He started laughing from behind his pile of smoke, and I laughed with him. "Hell, you're as crazy as old Trimble was. He apparently wised up, and that's when he stopped paying the premiums. Hell, son, no private citizen's going to set foot on the moon in our time."

"You're sure of that?"

"Sure?" he roared. "Sure? Of course, I'm sure."

"Then you'd let us pay up the back premiums and re-instate the policy?"

Derrickson's head popped out of the smoke again, and he pointed at me with his vile-smelling cigar. "Of course," he said. "Why not?"

"Well, that's fine. How much are the back premiums?"

Derrickson leaned back against the smoke, and it swallowed him. "Five hundred dollars a year," he said.

"And the policy lapsed seven years ago?"

"That's right. If you want to bring it up to date, you'd have to give us thirty-five hundred dollars. And we'd like the next year's premium paid in advance. Four thousand total."

"Will you take my check?" I asked, reaching into my jacket instantly.

"Certainly. But there's no rush."

"Well, I'd like to get it off my mind. Don't like loose ends."

Derrickson pushed the smoke away from his face now that we were ready to pass the cash across the table. It fled before his big hands, and he said, "Just make it out to Derrick and Derrickson. Four thousand dollars."

He pressed the button on his intercom and shouted, "Bring the *Prince* Magazine records."

"Yes, sir."

He reached into his bottom drawer then and pulled out a printed form with the words POLICY RENEWAL stamped across the top. He sighed, unscrewed the top of his fountain pen, and said, "Soon as I sign this, you'll be fully covered again." He chuckled loudly. "Against a sudden trip to the moon."

I shoved the check at him eagerly, nodding. I glanced at my watch. "Well, if you'll just sign it," I said.

"Got to fill in a few items first. I'll need the records for that."

"Couldn't I give you the information you need?"

"Nope. Need the records." He sucked deeply on his cigar, annoyed when he discovered it was out. He put down the pen, lit the cigar again, and began driving all the oxygen from the room once more. In a few moments the redhead came in with the records.

"Sir . . ." she started.

"Just a moment, Miss Freeley."

She stood by the desk patiently, grinning at me. Derrickson peered through his billowing screen and quickly copied the information he needed.

"There," he said at last. "Now I'll put the old John Han—"

"Sir . . ." the redhead said again, and I was beginning to dislike her intensely.

"Just a moment, Miss Freeley," Derrickson said.

"Sir . . ."

"What the hell is it, Miss Freeley?"

I stared at the pen poised over the dotted line.

"Couldn't you sign . . ."

"I'm sorry, sir," the redhead said, "but I didn't mean to interrupt. It's just that the most *won*derful thing has happened!"

"What's that?" Derrickson said. He put the pen on the paper, a small dot of ink appearing under the point. He looked up expectantly.

"A man has just returned from the moon!" the redhead said excitedly.

Derrickson clamped down on his cigar and lifted the pen as if it were on fire. "WHAT?" he boomed.

"Yes, sir, it's in all the papers and on all the broadcasts. Amos Donald is his name. He's the cutest man you ever . . ."

Derrickson turned his chair toward me slowly, great plumes of smoke streaming from his nose and the corners of his mouth.

"You—knew—this," he said slowly.

"No, Mr. Derrickson, I didn't," I said brightly. "Comes as a complete surprise to me. Comes as a—"

"Get out!" he screamed. "Get out of here before I—"

"But, Mr. Derrickson . . ."

"Get out, you cheap fourflusher!"

"But . . ."

"Get out, you . . . you . . . grifter!"

I got up quickly and headed for the door, and behind me the redhead asked, "Did I say something, Mr. Derrickson."

She certainly had.

Amos Donald brought proof the next day. He also brought photographers and newspapermen, and the offices of *Prince* were more crowded that they'd been in many a moo—many a day.

He lay the items on the desk one by one.

"Exhibit A," he said. "Gypsum. Taken from the moon."

"How do we know?" John asked.

"Have your scientists test it. Ain't no atmosphere on the moon. No erosion. No weathering. Have them test it against earth specimens. Absolutely authentic."

"Exhibit A," I said wearily.

"Exhibit B—silver. Got it on the moon, too." He plunked a piece of silver as big as my head onto the desk.

"Exhibit B," John said.

Mr. Donald lifted a bag. It was a big bag, and he needed both hands to raise it to the desk. Abruptly he turned it over, spilling the contents onto the mahogany.

"Exhibit C—moon pumice. Got it from Archimedes. Genuine article, believe me."

I looked at John, and John looked at me. We were both thinking of the $21,456.31 in *Prince's* treasury. That was a far cry from a million dollars. A far, far cry.

Mr. Donald opened a suitcase and brought out a bulky nylon and rubber contrivance. "Space suit I wore on the moon," he said quietly. The reporters began to buzz, and a few flash guns flashed. I looked at the space suit and at the helmet resting in the deep suitcase.

"Got two of 'em," Mr. Donald said. "One's a spare. Got that one over in the ship."

"The *what?*" I asked.

"Why, the ship. The one I went up with," Mr. Donald explained. "Had to have a ship, you know."

"Sure," John said, nodding. "He had to have a ship, Bert."

"Yes, of course."

"I was saving that 'til last," Mr. Donald said. "That's Exhibit B."

"B?"

"Oh, sure, I got lots more to show you."

He started to show us, and the photographers had a field day. By the time he finished, there were more mineral and rock specimens on my desk than in the Geology Department of the Museum of Natural History. He claimed he'd got them all on the moon. He also claimed that some of the minerals were compounds peculiar to the moon's airless, waterless nature. He left with a crowd of reporters behind him, while John and I desperately called in the scientists who had volunteered to examine the loot.

John clapped me on the shoulder and said, "We're in this to the end, Bert. Together."

"I appreciate that, old man," I told him.

I thought I saw a tear in John's eye, but I wasn't sure.

There were tears in mine, though, when the scientists delivered their reports.

Their spokesman sniffed the air like a beagle and then announced, "There can be no question. We have seen no specimens such as these on earth. Coupled with the photographs Mr. Donald was good enough to—"

"The *what?* What? What did you say?"

"Photographs," the spokesman said. "The ones Mr. Donald took on the moon. He was good enough to send them to us directly. Figured they'd help us to reach a fair decision. Unquestionably valid, too. Our most powerful instruments could never have got such close-ups. Coupled with these photographs, as I was saying, there can be no reasonable doubt that Mr. Donald has indeed been to the moon." The spokesman cleared his throat. "We . . . ah . . . have a suggestion to make, Mr. Merrian."

"What's that?"

"Pay the man his million dollars."

Mr. Donald saved the spaceship for last. We insisted on seeing that privately, without the invasion of the press. He agreed because he was closer to the million dollars now. Besides, he wanted to put away the space suit and the assorted items that had served as exhibits. When he'd done that, hanging the space suit alongside the spare in a locker, and stowing the specimens, he showed us around the control room. "Only one of its kind in the world," he said proudly. "Took me twenty years to build it. Ain't another like it."

"It looks complicated," I said.

"Ain't," Mr. Donald answered. "Simplest thing in the world. Built an orbit calculator right into it, you see. Only wanted it to take me one place, and that was the moon. So all I got to do is set the year and the day of the month with these knobs here, and it automatically figures just where the moon is, and what the orbit to take the ship there would have to be. Then all I do is press that there firing stud, and the thing just goes up." He lifted his forefinger. "Right to the moon."

"It was easy then," John said.

"Easy as pie. Be just as easy to get to all the planets with this baby. Anyone could figure it."

"Well," I said, "I guess he gets the million bucks."

"I guess so," John agreed wearily.

"We'd better get back to the office, John. If you'll contact us tomorrow, Mr. Donald, we'll have your check waiting for you."

"You're sure now?"

"Oh, yes," I said. I grinned feebly. "Why not? You've convinced us."

Mr. Donald seemed happy now. He led us out of the control room and down the ramp. The rocket site was deserted, and blackness covered the sky as we walked toward the company's automobile.

"Sure lonely out here," John said.

"Has to be," Mr. Donald answered. "Blast-off, you know. Can't have people injured by the jet trail."

"Naturally not," I said.

"Uhm," John agreed.

We rode back to the city in silence.

At the office Mr. Donald stepped out of the car. "Hope you fellows have that check tomorrow," he said. "I aim to make another trip up there. Figure maybe I'll hop to Mars from the moon. Need supplies, though. Plenty. Part of the check will go for that."

"What about fuel?" John asked.

"Oh, got my tanks full already. I can make that next trip soon as I get the money to stock up."

I thought of the $21,456.31 in our paltry bank account, and I wondered how much supplies that would buy for Mr. Donald. John looked at me, and I knew he was thinking the same thing.

"Well, good night, Mr. Donald," I said.

"Night, fellas. See you tomorrow."

"Sure," John called after him.

John's eyes met mine for an instant, and we grinned at each other.

"But are we doing the right thing?" John asked two days later.

"Have we got a million bucks?"

"After the spending we did? Hell, we're lucky if we have a thousand."

"Then we're doing the right thing," I said simply.

"I guess so."

"When in doubt, run."

"Suppose he catches up."

"Never," I said. "He's an old man, more or less. Besides, we can go to a great many places."

"And we can always start another magazine," John said hopefully. "Somewhere."

"Sure. Nothing to worry about."

We sat back in the seats and stretched luxuriously.

There was a hold full of supplies, and tanks full of fuel, and Mr. Donald's space ship handled like a dream.

We sat back and watched the stars and the approaching moon.

HAPPY NEW YEAR, HERBIE

WE WERE LIVING on North Brother Island at the time.

It was, and is, a tiny island in the middle of the East River, adjacent to a miniscule uninhabited island called South Brother. When we lived there, and I suppose the same is true of it, now, the Riker's Island prison was visible in the distance from one end of the island, and from the opposite end, the Bronx mainland. There was a lot of river traffic passing North Brother. From our windows in one of the converted buildings we could see tugs and barges and transports and tankers and once even a Swedish luxury liner.

The buildings we lived in had once been part of a hospital for tuberculars, the hospital rooms converted into apartments shortly after the war. When Joan and I were first married, we lived in McCloskey Hall, which was on the end of the island opposite the tennis courts and the handball court and a sort of outdoor teahouse overlooking the edge of the river and Hell's Gate on the horizon. Later, just before our first son was born, we applied for and moved to a larger apartment on the other end of the island in a building called Finley Hall. If all of the buildings sounded like part of a college campus, it was with good reason. The island had initially been leased by Columbia, N.Y.U., and Fordham, I think, and was euphemistically called Riverside Campus or Riverside Extension or some such, the idea being to provide housing for World War II veterans who were attending these colleges. The unmarried students lived in a dormitory in the center of the island, the old administration building.

174

The married veterans and their wives lived in the converted hospital buildings. Later on, the accommodations were extended to include veterans from other colleges in the city and, toward the end, the island accepted veterans who were attending *any* school approved by the Veterans Administration—which is how Herbie came to live on North Brother. I say "toward the end" not because the island went up in smoke or anything like that, but simply because the buildings eventually reverted to what they'd been originally: a hospital. In the old days, before the students invaded it, the island had housed such medical phenomena as Typhoid Mary. After we left, it became the Riverside Hospital for drug addicts. We, the interim students, were only a part of its brief, non-medical history.

Our apartment in Finley Hall was at the end of a long corridor on the fourth floor. The original hospital rooms had been revamped so that there were five apartments on each floor, the apartments varying in size according to the families occupying them. The smallest apartment on each floor was a single rectangular room that had once been the old hospital elevator shaft. On our floor it was shared by Peter, who was a dental student, and his wife Gerry, who listened to the radio wearing earphones so as not to disturb her husband while he studied.

Our own apartment was slightly larger than the converted elevator shaft. It consisted of two rooms and a john. The door opened on an enormous living room-dining room-kitchen combined, with windows facing the river north and south. Joan and I slept in the living room on a bed that doubled as a sofa during the day. The other room was smaller, with windows facing the river on the west, and Timmy—our new-born son—slept in that room, The bathroom was tacked onto one end of Timmy's room. We decorated the bathroom with covers from *Collier's* Magazine pasted to the wallboard, even though someone told us we'd lose our original security deposit if we papered the walls. But aside from this single effort, there wasn't much else we could do to improve the apartment. It had been hastily reconstructed in a time when new housing was practically nonexistent in New York. The paint was thin; the plasterboard showed through in uneven patches, and even the nails holding plasterboard to stud were clearly visible. The floors were presumably the original asphalt tile that had run through the old hospital. You could still see marks on the tile where entire walls had been ripped out in the transformation. The river moisture kept the apartment constantly damp, and the closed cupboards over the sink were a haven for cockroaches, no matter how many forays Joan and I made into their territory with insecticide powders and sprays. The view was magnificent, of course, and perhaps if we'd had any money we could have framed the view elegantly. But we were students living on my G.I. allotment and on what Joan and I could earn with part-time jobs. Joan had dropped out of school just before Timmy was born, and I was in my senior year and working after school each day at the World Student Service Fund on West Fortieth Street and on Sundays at the Y as a counselor. On Saturdays, Joan went to her job in the music department at Macy's while I stayed home to wash and wax the old asphalt-tile floor, change Timmy's diapers, and continue my sworn and unceasing guerrilla warfare against the goddamn cockroaches. Joan had been a music major at Hunter College, which is how she'd got the job at Macy's. We'd been engaged for two years when we heard about North Brother Island and decided to get married immediately. I guess we'd both thought of marriage as having friends in for coffee, or of putting our laundry into a washing machine together, or of planning menus for the week. At least, our idea was to continue living in McCloskey Hall until we were both graduated and then go to Paris for a year where I would learn to write and Joan would continue with her studies at the Conservatory or someplace. But we were married in October, and on New Year's Eve of that first year on the island Timmy was conceived. And suddenly we were married in earnest and not on an extended honeymoon, and shortly after that we were parents to boot. It was our second New Year's Eve on the island, when we were living in Finley, that the thing happened with Herbie.

In a sense, despite our new responsibilities, our stay on the island *was* an extended honeymoon. We were surrounded by students or recent graduates who were just as broke as we were. The island was reached by a ferryboat that shuttled back and forth at unpredictable times, often carrying handcuffed convicts to Riker's Island as its second stop. There were hardly any automobiles on the island; you could walk from one end of it to the other in less than five minutes. On a still autumn night, even after Timmy was born, we would go outside with other married college students and play charades or even hide-and-seek. The island was peacefully quiet, and you could hear a baby if he so much as turned in his crib. On Sunday nights they would show old movies in the rec hall, stuff like *Citizen Kane* and *Pinocchio* and *The Philadelphia Story*. Admission was twenty-five cents a head, and Joan and I would take turns running up to check on Timmy every time the projectionist stopped to change a reel, unless we'd arranged for Peter and Gerry to look in on him. We used to keep our money in a little tin box divided into compartments, so much a week for rent, so much for transportation, so much for entertainment. I can remember a night when Joan wept herself to sleep because she'd backed a straight flush in a poker game and lost our three-dollar entertainment allotment to someone with a royal flush. The island was literally an island, but it was also a figurative never-never land that was a part of the city and yet removed from it. It was, in a sense, a country club for paupers.

Herbie moved into the apartment alongside ours just before Christmas. His wife's name was Shirley, and they had a son and a daughter, both under three years of age. Herbie was studying to be a television repairman. It is perhaps difficult to imagine snobbery among paupers, but the old-timers on the island strongly resented the new rules that allowed the admission of men going to upholstery schools, or television-repair schools, or even barbers' colleges. Many of the old island residents were men and women working for their master's degrees; some were going for their doctorates; most considered it beneath the dignity of the island to accept people who were not, by their standards, bona fide students. I wish I could say that Joan and I were unaffected by such petty considerations, but the truth is we felt as put upon as any of the others. The island was our neighborhood, our private retreat from the city. And now our neighborhood was getting run-down. We discussed it with our friends often and vehemently, and when Herbie and his wife moved into the apartment alongside ours and across the hall from Peter and Gerry, we unanimously felt there was now more to cope with than the indestructible cockroaches. And yet I don't think this resentment had anything to do with what happened on New Year's Eve. Or maybe it did; I simply don't know. I do know that Joan and I could have continued living on the island for many months after New Year's Eve and before it was reconverted to a hospital, but we applied for rooms in a city housing project instead. We left the island in March and never again saw any of the people who had been at the party that night.

I don't remember whose idea the party was. I think it was Jason's. It seems reasonable to assume this, because most of the ideas in Finley Hall, if not on the entire island, seemed to originate with Jason. I think he mentioned it casually just before Christmas while someone was serving eggnog laced with rum. I think it was only a drunken suggestion at first, "Let's have a New Year's Eve party," and then someone else said, "Why not?" and then Norman picked it up wholeheartedly—but yes, I'm sure the original suggestion was Jason's. And it must have been in his apartment at the other end of the fourth floor, facing inland, yes, and Mary had just put one of the kids to bed. They had at least a dozen kids in that small apartment. Well, actually they had only three, but even this was considerable when you realized Jason had only been out of Columbia for a year. He'd begun working at an advertising agency almost immediately upon graduation but was still taking some night courses, a dodge many of the married students used to maintain their eligibility for the low-rent island apartments. Mary didn't look like the mother of three children, or for that matter like the mother of even one child. In fact, Mary seemed to echo the fantasy that was North Brother Island, walking around with a three-year-old by her side, a two-year-old on her hip, and an infant in a carriage, and looking freckled and innocent and virginal in her sloppy sweaters and scuffed loafers, as if she had just wandered out of Julia Richman High School. Joan told me that Mary had called her to the window one afternoon shortly after we'd moved in, when Joan was in her eighth month and as big as a house, and had said, "Joan, will you come down and play with me?" She thought it odd that a woman with three children should be asking another grown woman—we all thought of ourselves as grownups then—to come down and play with her, but it seemed to me thoroughly appropriate for the woman who was married to Jason.

It was, in fact, impossible to imagine Jason in any conceivable world outside North Brother Island. The concept of him leaving the island to enter a city full of people earning their daily bread was almost laughable, and yet he did it every weekday morning, and with an earnestness that bordered on fanaticism. It was Jason who once leaped over the metal railing onto the deck of the ferry as it pulled away from the island. It was Jason who, on another morning, ran down to the dock in his pajamas, his working clothes slung over his arm, and then washed and dressed in the men's room before the boat reached the mainland. It was Jason who knew everyone on the island by his first name, Jason who first suggested we play hide-and-seek one night, Jason who discovered and used the outdoor barbecue near the teahouse looking out at Hell's Gate.

I had seen Jason often on the ferry while we were still living in McCloskey Hall. He was a tall, strikingly handsome man with black hair and blue eyes that seemed always smiling. His closest friend was a fellow named Norman who lived on the third floor of Finley Hall, a tall blond man with an excellent build and the same laughing look in his gray eyes. They would walk onto the ferry together, talking and joking, and then would go to sit in the bow of the boat where they were immediately surrounded by a half-dozen people who seemed to be having the time of their lives each morning. Sitting on the bench with an open book in my lap, hearing the sounds of laughter from the bow, I felt the unconscious pang of the outsider and longed for a moment to be a part of such obvious good fellowship.

I did not become a part of it until late August, when we had already moved into Finley Hall and were awaiting the birth of the baby. The first hurricane of the year came about three days before Joan expected to go to the hospital. I had been a New Yorker all my life and was used to the hurricane season, but I had never lived through a hurricane on an island in the middle of the East River with my wife momentarily expecting a baby. There was a cyclone fence around the entire island, and the water rose above that until the fence was no longer visible, and then the water covered the outdoor wash lines, and then it flooded into Finley Hall and began rising in the basement of the building. The radio was warning all residents of the city to tape windows and lash down anything that might be blown away, and the Coast Guard advised all residents of North Brother that it was standing by to take people to the mainland. The big question for everyone living in Finley, considering the fact that this was only the prelude to the storm, with the worst expected later in the afternoon, was whether or not to leave with the Coast Guard. The question was enormously magnified for me because I had visions of Joan suddenly going into labor at the height of the storm. We were debating whether or not to accept the Coast Guard's offer when we suddenly heard a drum beating somewhere in the building. We both went into the hall.

Jason was standing on the ground-floor landing, the water already up to his knees. He was wearing a yellow rubber rain cape and sou'wester, and he was beating a huge drum and shouting, "Hear ye, hear ye," while Norman read off a proclamation. The proclamation stated that the residents of Finley Hall refused to be intimidated by the elements but instead chose to defend their homes in the teeth of the storm. It went on to imply strongly that anyone who left the building was, in effect, a rat deserting the sinking ship. There was, I must admit, an element of adventure to what Jason proposed. He wanted every able-bodied man to come immediately to the ground floor, where the furniture of the occupants there would be moved to a higher level just in case the water continued to rise. He then wanted a task force to go through the entire building, taping windows, making sure that cribs were protected from possible shattering glass, seeing that flashlights and kerosene lamps were available to each and every person who chose to remain.

I turned to Joan. "What do you think?" I asked.

There was a worried look on Joan's face. I now realize she was scared to death of having her first baby, terrified by the prospect of not being able to reach the hospital should she go into labor. I mistook her fear for the indecision of a nineteen-year-old. She turned to me; she turned to the strong guidance of her twenty-one-year-old husband. "Whatever you think," she said.

"Well, how do you feel?"

"I feel all right."

"Then let's stay, okay?"

Joan nodded doubtfully. "Okay," she said.

Under the leadership of Jason, we worked tirelessly all that afternoon, moving furniture, taping windows, and then sitting through the silence that came with the eye of the storm. The funny part was that the storm dissipated entirely. We were all awaiting the onslaught with a cheerful adventurousness that belied the actual danger. Looking from the fourth-floor window, it was impossible to tell where the island ended and the river began. Finley Hall rose like a tall white finger out of the waves, its basement and ground floor already flooded, the water halfway up the steps to the first floor. We had worked hard, and afterward Jason rewarded us with drinks in his apartment while we waited for the real storm to strike.

Instead, it blew out to sea.

I can still remember the slightly embarrassed faces of the people who had left the island and who returned the next morning, carrying their precious belongings. By then, I felt I was becoming one of Jason's friends, and I was able to share his laughter and his pointed gibes. The next day I took Joan to the hospital and Timmy was born.

I don't know how other people feel when they are presented with their first son. I now have three sons, and Timmy is almost thirteen years old, but I was twenty-one when he was born and a senior in college, and my pride at the time was mixed with a sense of unreality. I was a father; I could look through the plate-glass window at the hospital and see the red-faced infant they said was mine, but I honestly did not *feel* like a father. I felt instead as though I were only going through the time-honored motions of passing out cigars, of inviting Jason and Norman in for drinks, in an attempt to convince myself— without real conviction—that I was honestly a father. Jason, on the other hand, was my idea of what a parent should be. He was, after all, the father of three children, and yet he had never lost his youthfulness or his joy for living. I would watch him running through the hallway with his two eldest, firing toy guns at them, entering their world wholeheartedly, falling dead over the banister when one of his sons fired an imaginary bullet. I would watch him parading around the island with his infant daughter perched on his shoulders, pointing out the boats on the river, or the sunset, talking to her in a childish prattle that I'm sure to this day she understood. It seemed to me that this was the sort of relationship I wanted with my son. It seemed to me that Jason had managed to hang onto a marvelous capacity for finding fun in everything, and I was determined to follow his good example.

In October we had our peeping Tom. In the middle of the night we heard a scream from the other end of the hallway, and then Jason was yelling something, and I leaped out of bed and ran to the door. Jason and Mary were already in the hallway, and Norman was running up from the third floor in his pajamas, shouting, "Jason? What is it? What's the matter?" Mary was wearing a baby-doll nightgown and no robe, but there was nothing provocative about her as she stood in the hallway behind Jason; she looked instead like a twelve-year-old who had been startled out of sleep by a bad dream. The dream, it seemed, was real enough. She had been nursing her daughter when she chanced to look up at the window and saw a man's face looking in at her. She had screamed and then covered her breast, and Jason had begun shouting at the man, and here we were now, standing in the chilly hallway in our pajamas, confronted with what looked like a very serious situation. We all knew there were unmarried students on the island, and it seemed to us now that one of them was possibly a pervert. It was four o'clock in the morning, and time for Timmy's bottle, so we all went into our apartment and Joan made some coffee while I warmed the bottle, and then while I fed Timmy we discussed what we were going to do about our peeping Tom.

There was a feeling of warmth and unity in our kitchen that early morning, generated by the close friendship between Norman and Jason, the concern Norman showed for poor Mary. We sat drinking hot, steaming coffee, not at all frightened by what had happened to Mary, sweet Mary who looked like a high-school girl in her sweaters and skirts, but determined instead to find the intruder. We had no idea what we would do with him once we captured him, nor do I think any one of us was thinking in terms of punishment. The important thing was to catch him, and it became clear almost immediately that the chase, rather than the capture, would hold all the excitement.

There was no fire escape outside the window where the man's face had appeared. The windows on the inland side were high up on the wall, like elongated slits in a turret. Mary was sure the face had been hanging at her window upside down, so it seemed likely that the man had simply crawled to the edge of the roof and then leaned far out and over to peer in at her. To confirm our suspicions, Norman went for a flashlight and we climbed the six steps from the fourth floor to the roof. We found that the lock on the roof door had been broken open. In our pajamas we walked to the edge of the roof directly above Mary's window. We found a discarded candy wrapper there, a sure sign to us that someone had recently been there.

Jason was bursting with plans. It never occurred to any of us to wonder how our peeping Tom had known Mary would be nursing her baby at exactly four o'clock in the morning. We listened as Jason—who had been an ensign during the war   outlined a watch schedule for every man in Finley Hall on a rotating basis throughout the nights to follow. Norman loved the idea, and he devised an intricate alarm system, with each man in the building assigned a post to which he would hurry should our lookout sound the call.

We put the schedule into effect the following night.

There were twenty-two men living in Finley Hall at the time, five on each floor, and two on the ground-floor landing. We exempted from watch Peter, the dental student, because he was studying for exams—he was, it seemed to me, *always* studying for exams—and also a man named Mike on the second floor because he was holding a nighttime job as well as attending classes during the day. That left twenty men among whom to divide the ten P.M. to six A.M. watch schedule. We decided that a two-hour watch would be long enough for men who were expected to be bright and attentive the next morning. With twenty men available, this meant that each of us would stand watch once every five days. Actually I only got to stand two watches, one from midnight to two A.M., and the other from two A.M. to four A.M., before we called the whole thing off.

We never did catch our intruder; I'm not sure we were trying very hard. Besides, word of our vigilance spread all over the island, and our man would have been a fool to pay a return visit. But Jason's idea was a rewarding one nonetheless. We had all been subjected either to watches or guard duty during our time in the service, but this was somehow different. It was October, and not too cold, and there was something almost pioneerlike about setting the alarm and waking in the middle of the night, touching Joan's warm shoulder where she lay asleep in the sofa bed, and then going up to the roof where Norman was waiting to be relieved. Each night Mary provided a thermos of hot coffee for the men standing watch. Norman would hand over the flashlight, and I would pour myself a cup and then lean against the parapet wall, alone, looking up at the stars or out over the river. There was a lot of sky over North Brother Island. The stars were sharp and bright against it; the air was crisp. The factories on the mainland burned with activity all night, their long stacks sending up pillars of gray smoke tinted with the glow of neon. The prison on Riker's Island was dark except for probing fingers of light that occasionally pierced the blackness. There was hardly any river traffic, no hooting of tugs, no pounding diesels. Out on the dark water you could hear only the solemn gonging of the buoy marking South Brother Island and beneath that, if you listened very carefully, the gentle hiss of waves slipping almost soundlessly against the walls of the island.

I thought a lot of things alone on the roof of Finley Hall. I wondered about the future and about what was in store for Joan and me and our newborn son. I thought ahead to graduation; I thought of our canceled Paris sojourn, perhaps lost to us forever. I thought a lot about marriage and about what my responsibilities were supposed to be. The night encouraged speculation. I was twenty-one years old, and the world lay ahead of me, and I searched the darkness for answers it could not and did not contain.

That was in October.

In December, Herbie and Shirley and their two children moved into the building. I must describe them now as they first seemed to me and not as I came to see them later, after New Year's Eve. They were, to begin with, much older than most of the people on the island. Herbie was perhaps thirty-eight, and his wife was at least thirty-five. We were not still young enough to believe that anyone past thirty was middle-aged, but Herbie and Shirley were certainly beyond us in years, and this made them strangers to us. Then, too, they were from someplace in the Middle West; he had chosen to be discharged in New York City so that he could go to television school there before going back home with his family. So, in addition to their age, they spoke with an accent that was unfamiliar to most of us and grating on the ears. But, most important, Herbie and Shirley were not attractive people. He was short and stout and always seemed to have a beard stubble, even immediately after he had shaved. He was nearsighted and wore thick spectacles that magnified his eyes to almost Martian proportions. He was balding at the back of his head, unevenly, so that he always seemed in need of a haircut. He wore brown shoes with a blue suit, and he moved with a lumbering, ponderous gait that seemed designed to infuriate speedier people. His wife seemed to be a perfect soul mate. She called him "Herbert," and she looked at him with adoring eyes that were a pale, washed-out blue in a shapeless plain face. She had borne two children and apparently never bothered with post-natal exercises; her figure, like her face, was shapeless, and she draped it with clothes in the poorest taste. She made only one concession to beauty, and that was in the form of a home bleach job on her hair, which left it looking like lifeless straw. Watching them walk to the ferry together was like watching a comic vaudeville routine. You always expected one or the other of them to take a pratfall, and when neither did, it only heightened their comic effect.

The walls on North Brother Island were hastily erected and paper-thin; Herbie and his wife lived in the apartment immediately next door to ours. It was impossible not to hear them in the middle of the night.

"Herbert," she would say, "Do you think I'm beautiful?"

"I think you're very beautiful," Herbie would answer in his thick Midwestern voice.

"Do you think I have a good figure?"

"I think you have a beautiful figure, Shirley."

There would be a pause. Joan and I would lie motionless on our sofa bed. The night was still.

"Herbert, do you love me?"

"I love you, darling. I love you."

Joan got out of bed one night and whispered, "I don't want to listen. Please, do we have to listen?"

"Honey, what can we do?" I whispered back.

"I don't know. I'm going into Timmy's room. I don't want to listen. I think . . . " She shook her head. "It makes me feel that maybe we sound that way, too."

We went into Timmy's room. He was sleeping peacefully, his blond head turned into the pillow. We sat together in the old easy chair near his crib, Joan on my lap, her head on my shoulder. We sat quietly for a long time. The December winds raced over the river and shuddered against the windows in the small room.

Her mouth close to my ear, Joan whispered, "Are you very angry with me?"

"About what?"

"Paris. About not going."

"No," I said, but I suppose my voice could not hide my disappointment.

"I didn't want a baby so soon, you know," she said.

"I know, darling."

"But I do love him. He seems so helpless. Doesn't he seem helpless to you?"

"I suppose so."

"Do you wonder about us?" Joan asked.

"Sometimes."

"I do. A lot. I sometimes feel . . . I don't know . . . I feel we never talk to each other much any more, the way we used to when we were single." She paused. She was silent for a very long time. Then she said, "I don't want to get lost."

"We won't get lost."

"I don't want to get lost in people."

"We won't."

"I feel so . . . so terribly afraid that . . ." She shook her head.

"What is it, darling?"

"I have the feeling I never finished being a girl," she whispered, "and now I have to be a woman. I don't know what to do. Sometimes I feel like sitting on the dock where the ferry comes in and just let my feet hang in the water, and then I remember I'm a mother now and can't do that, but at the same time everything here seems so . . . as if, well, as if I could do that and nobody would mind very much or even notice it." She paused again. "I'm going to say something terrible."

"What?"

"I wish we hadn't had the baby." She took a deep breath. "I wish we could have gone to Paris."

"We'll go one day," I whispered.

"Will it matter then?" she said, and she began weeping softly against my shoulder, and I could feel her trembling in my arms. In a little while we went back to bed. The apartment next door was silent.

    ✿   ✿   ✿

My first real encounter with Herbie came shortly after Christmas. Joan's mother had given us a television set as a present, and I was busy at the pay telephone on the second-floor landing of Finley when Herbie came lumbering up the steps. I guess he couldn't help overhearing my conversation, which was with a television man, and which concerned the price of putting up an antenna and installing the set. He lingered awhile at the top of the landing, and when I hung up, he asked, "How much does he want?"

"Too much," I said.

Herbie smiled. There was a sweetness to his smile that contradicted his absurd appearance and his horrible speech. He offered his smile the way some men offer their hands for a handshake, openly and without guile.

"I'd be happy to do it for you," he said.

"What do you mean?"

"Put up the antenna, take care of the installation."

"Well, thanks," I said, "but I think . . ."

"I know how," Herbie said.

"Well, I'm sure you do, but . . ."

"I mean, in case you didn't think I knew how."

"I just wouldn't want to impose on your time, Herbie."

"Be no imposition at all. I'd be happy to do it."

I was trying to figure how I could possibly tell Herbie I would prefer paying for a professional job, even if it meant paying more than I would have to pay him for the installation, when he suddenly said, "I didn't mean to charge you, you know."

"What?"

"All you'd have to do would be pay for the parts, that's all. I'd be happy to put it up for the experience alone."

"Well . . ."

Herbie smiled gently. "None of us have too much money to throw around, I guess."

"I couldn't let you do that," I said.

"You'd be doing me a great favor," Herbie answered.

So that Saturday I went up to the roof with Herbie to put up the television antenna. It took me about five minutes to realize I wasn't needed at all, but I went on with the pretense of helping anyway, handing Herbie a tool every now and then, holding the antenna erect while he put the straps around the chimney, generally offering needless assistance. We'd been up there for about a half hour when Jason and Norman joined us. They were both wearing old Navy foul-weather jackets, the wind whipping their hair into their eyes.

"Well, now, that's a pretty good job, Herbie," Jason said.

Herbie, tightening the wire straps around the chimney, smiled gently and said, "Thank you."

"How long have you been going to that school of yours?" Norman asked.

"Oh, just two months." Herbie shrugged apologetically. "This isn't too hard to learn, you know."

"Do you like doing it?" I asked.

"Oh, yes, I love it," Herbie said.

Jason looked at Norman with a smile on his face and then turned to Herbie again. "Were you involved with electronics in the service?" he asked.

"Oh, no," Herbie said without looking up. He was retightening each wire strap until I felt sure the chimney brick would crumble. "I was a small-arms instructor at Fort Dix."

"That right?" Jason said, a curious lilt to his voice.

Herbie laughed. "I think I was taken by mistake. My eyes are terrible, you know."

"No!" Jason said, in mock surprise. "*Your* eyes? I don't believe it."

I looked at Jason curiously because I suddenly realized he was riding Herbie, and I couldn't see why, nor did I think it was very nice to ride a guy who was doing me a favor and saving me money. But Herbie didn't catch the inflection of Jason's voice. He went right on tightening the wire straps, and he laughed a little and said, "Oh, sure, I've been wearing these thick glasses ever since I was a kid. But, I don't know, the doctor who examined me said I was okay, so they drafted me." He shrugged. Cheerfully he added, "They used to call me Cockeye when I was a kid."

"How'd you like the Army?" I asked.

"I thought I was going to be a hero," Herbie said musingly. "Me, a hero. Wiping out German machine-gun nests, things like that, you know? Instead, the minute I got in, they took one look and realized just how blind I really was. They figured if they sent me over to fight, I'd be shooting at the wrong army all the time. So they made me an instructor." He shrugged. "After a while I began to enjoy it. I like taking things apart and putting them together again."   .

"Then television ought to be right up your alley," Jason said.

"Sure," Herbie agreed. He stepped back from the chimney and surveyed his work. "There, that ought to hold it. We get some pretty strong winds on this end of the island."

He walked away from the chimney and began paying out a roll of narrow wire to the edge of the roof. He worked with an intense concentration, a faint smile flickering on his mouth, as if he were pleased to see that things he'd learned in theory were actually capable of being put into practice.

"So you never got to be a hero, huh, Herbie?" Norman said, and his voice carried the same peculiar mocking tone as Jason's.

"I guess not," Herbie said, smiling. He shrugged. "But it's just a matter of coming to grips, isn't it?"

"Isn't *what?*" Norman said.

"All of it. All of life. Coming to grips, that's all." He shrugged. "When I was a kid, I used to cry in my pillow because they called me Cockeye. One night I threw my glasses on the floor and then stepped on them and broke them in a million pieces. Only that didn't change anything. I was still cockeyed in the morning, only worse because I didn't have my glasses."

"I don't see what that has to do with being a hero," Jason said.

"Well, some guys never get to be heroes. I'm not so sure it's important."

"It might be," Jason said.

"You think so? I don't know. I keep asking myself what does Nappanee, Indiana, really need? A hero or a television repairman?" He grinned. "I think they need a television repairman."

"Maybe they need a hero, too," Jason said, and it suddenly seemed to me he was taking this all very personally, though I couldn't for the life of me see why.

"Maybe," Herbie admitted. "Listen, I think it would be very nice to be a television repairman *and* a hero. All I'm saying is that I'm happy to be what I am."

"Which is what, Herbie?"

Herbie looked up from the roll of wire, surprised, turning his face toward Jason. The glasses reflected the sky overhead, giving his eyes a curiously opaque look. "Why, *me*," he said. "That's all. Me." He cocked his head and continued to look at Jason in puzzlement. "Look, I'm going to be cockeyed for the rest of my life, there's nothing going to change that. But I look at my kid's faces, I look into their eyes, I say to myself, Thank God, you've got good clear eyes and can see for twenty miles." He shrugged. "That's all."

"I think I'm missing your point, Herbie," Jason said.

"I'm not trying to make any point," Herbie said amiably. "I'm only saying that part of living is sooner or later you come to grips. You look around you and decide what's important, that's all. It's important to me that my kids have good eyes. That's more important to me than all the German machine-gun nests in the world." He walked to the edge of the roof and looked over. "Let's go down and hook this thing up, okay?" he said.

Jason hesitated a moment, glanced at Norman, and then smiled. "Herbie," he said slowly and evenly, "the tenants in the building are having a party on New Year's Eve. It'll be fun. Would you and Shirley like to come?"

Herbie turned from the edge of the roof. The sky was still reflected in his thick glasses, and the smile that covered his face was curiously eyeless.

"We'd love to," he said softly. "Thank you very much."

I suppose the party began to go wrong while it was still in its planning stages, though none of us seemed to recognize it at the time. We were all living on very tight budgets, and whereas we wanted to have our party, we didn't want to have it at the expense of going hungry for the next month. It was decided almost immediately that everyone would bring his own bottle and that the party fund would provide setups. There was no disagreement on this point because it meant that each guest could bring and consume as much liquor as he desired without putting undue financial stress on the light drinkers in the building. Joan and I had hardly progressed beyond the two-drinks-an-evening stage of our social development, so we naturally were all for such an arrangement.

But all agreement seemed to end right there, and the party committee, of which I was a member, must have met at least four times between Christmas and New Year's Eve in an attempt to find a solution acceptable to all. The biggest areas of disagreement concerned food and decorations. There were members of the committee, and they presumably spoke for others in the building, who maintained that neither food nor decorations were necessary elements of a good party and that it would be foolish to waste money on them. The strongest proponent of this line of thought was Norman, whose wife was pregnant and who was undoubtedly trying to save every penny he could. If we'd gone along with his reasoning, the party would have cost him only the price of his own bottle, plus whatever we decided to chip in for setups. But Jason argued, with my firm support, that it wouldn't be New Year's Eve without food and balloons and confetti and noise-makers and hats. Norman countered by saying a good party was only a collection of people, and Jason squelched him by suggesting we didn't even need liquor if a good party was only a good collection of people.

"We're paying for our *own* liquor!" Norman said heatedly.

"Yes, which is exactly why we should all chip in for decorations and food."

"No," Norman said. "In the first place . . ."

"Ah, come on, Norman," I put in. "If everyone drinks all night without any food, we'll get sick."

"We'll get drunk," Norman said, "not *sick*."

"We've got to have *something* in our stomachs," Jason argued.

"Then eat *before* you come to the party!"

"The thing'll go on for hours. We're bound to get hungry again."

"Then bring your own food."

"That's ridiculous. It'll be cheaper if we all chip in for it."

"Why should we?" Norman said. "All I want to do is drink and celebrate New Year's Eve, so why should I chip in for food?"

"I think we ought to put it to a vote," Jason said.

We voted, and it was decided that each couple coming to the party would chip in five dollars for food, setups, and decorations. Norman was in a rage. He was Jason's closest friend, and this must have seemed like outright villainy to him. He had voted vehemently against the motion, and now he sulked in a corner for several moments and then said, "Well, *I'm* not chipping in for all that stuff."

"What do you mean?" Jason asked.

"Just what I said. If that's the price of admission, count me out."

"It's not the price of admission. We just want to make sure—"

"Then can I pay for the setups alone?"

"Well . . ."

"Oh, don't worry. I won't eat any of your food or touch your noisemakers or hats."

"You want me to lend you five dollars?" Jason asked.

"I don't need your five dollars, thanks. It's not the money, it's the principle."

"What are you going to do?" Jason asked. "Just sit there with your wife while we all stuff ourselves?"

"We won't be hungry. We won't touch your food," Norman said with dignity.

With equal dignity Jason replied, "You are entirely welcome to come to the party, *and* to use our noisemakers and hats, *and* to eat our food. You are entirely welcome, Norman, whether you choose to pay the five dollars or not."

"If I don't pay, I won't eat," Norman said.

"And you won't make any noise, either, right?"

"I don't need noisemakers to make noise. God invented voices before he invented noisemakers."

"God invented tightwads, too, before he invented—"

"Now look, Jason," Norman said angrily, "don't go calling me a—"

"I apologize," Jason said angrily. "Are you coming to the party or not?"

"I'm coming to the party!" Norman shouted.

New Year's Eve that year was a cold and dismal night. The windowpanes in Timmy's room were frosted with ice, and we hung blankets over them to keep the cold away from his crib. Both Joan and I dressed in the kitchen near the radiator on the south wall. I wore my blue suit, and she put on the black dress she had worn to her college junior prom. I had mixed a plastic container full of orange juice and then poured some gin into it, and we expected that to last us the entire evening. We were about to go out of the apartment when Joan stopped me. She put her hands on my shoulders and reached up and very tenderly kissed me on the mouth and then whispered, "Happy new year, darling."

"It'll be a good year," I said, and Joan smiled and took my arm and we went out into the hallway. Herbie and Shirley were just coming out of their apartment next door. He was wearing a gray pin-stripe double-breasted suit that looked as if it had belonged to his father. Shirley was wearing black, and there was an orchid pinned to the waist of her dress. She smiled a bit shyly and said, "Herbert brings me an orchid every New Year's." Joan and I nodded in approval, and the four of us walked together to Jason's apartment at the end of the hall. The door was open, and the record player that Peter, the dental student, had provided was going full blast. We had worked in the apartment all that afternoon, moving furniture into the other room, leaving behind only chairs, a stand for the record player, and a long table, trying to clear the small room so that people could dance if they wanted to. Jason's three kids had been deposited in an apartment on the third floor—it would have been Norman's apartment had they not argued so vehemently before the party—and so were in no danger of being awakened by the revelries. We had strung crepe paper across the room and draped it with confetti streamers and balloons. Joan hadn't seen the results of our labor until we walked into the apartment, and she smiled now and squeezed my arm and said, "It looks marvelous."

There were perhaps twenty people in the apartment when we got there, with another ten expected, the rest of the tenants having made other plans for the night before the idea for the party presented itself. No one was dancing as yet, but there was a lively buzz in the room, and drinks were being poured freely, and the long table was set with the ham and turkey we'd bought, and several loaves of bread, and potato chips and pretzels, and celery and carrots, and it all looked very nice and warm and I began to have the feeling this was going to be one of the best New Year's Eves I'd ever spent. I poured drinks for Joan and myself from the plastic container, and then I set the container down on the table and asked Joan to dance, and Jason yelled, "There they go, they're breaking the ice!" and everyone laughed. But we were indeed breaking the ice, because Herbie and Shirley followed us onto the floor almost immediately, and several other couples joined us, and pretty soon everyone was dancing with the exception of Jason and Mary, who stood in the doorway to the other room, watching us with pleasant smiles on their faces, and Peter and Gerry, who seemed to have discovered each other after a long siege of struggling with teeth and were talking and laughing as if they'd just been introduced. It took me several moments to realize that Norman and his wife weren't in the room. I looked at my watch. It was only ten-thirty, which wasn't too late, considering this was New Year's Eve, but I began to wonder whether or not Norman would show up. And then, as if in answer to my question, Norman and his wife Alice appeared in the doorway, smiling and carrying a bottle of Scotch, and they walked immediately to a pair of chairs opposite the long table set with food, far away from the table, clear over on the other side of the room, and promptly poured themselves drinks and began drinking.

"Well, let's eat," Jason said suddenly, and I turned to look at him, because it was only ten thirty, and many of the guests hadn't shown up yet, and besides, most of us had had late dinners in anticipation of the evening. But there he was, moving toward the table and beginning to slice the ham.

"It's a little early, isn't it, Jason?" I said, smiling.

"I just want to keep up my strength," Jason answered. "It's going to be a long night," and he continued to pile ham and turkey into a sandwich and then bit into it hungrily and smacked his lips and said, "Mmm, that's good," while Norman watched him from the other side of the room with a tight little smile on his mouth.

I don't think Norman or Alice budged from their chairs all night long. They sat opposite the table piled with food, and they made their keen displeasure felt by their presence, sitting like a pair of shocked chaperones witnessing an orgy. I didn't go near the table, and neither did a lot of other people, simply because Norman kept watching it with that small smile on his face, his eyes getting more and more glazed as he drank more and more Scotch. Jason, on the other hand, kept visiting the table as if it were a free lunch counter, eating like a glutton and smacking his lips with each bite he took, urging Mary to eat, pressing food on anyone who danced by, and finally picking up the tray with the turkey on it and carrying it across the room to where Norman and Alice sat, getting quietly and angrily drunk.

"Won't you have some turkey, Norman?" he asked sweetly. "Alice?"

"Thank you, I'm not hungry," Norman said.

"It's eleven forty-five," Jason answered. "Come on, have a bite."

"Thank you," Alice said sweetly, "we had a late dinner."

"Why, Norman," Jason said, "you're not wearing a party hat. This is New Year's Eve. Mary, bring Norman a party hat."

"I don't need a party hat," Norman said.

"*Everybody* needs a party hat," Jason said.

"Not *me*," Norman answered firmly.

"Then have a balloon," Jason said, and he put the turkey tray down on a chair and reached up for a balloon and then suddenly pushed the balloon against the lighted end of Norman's cigarette. The balloon exploded, and Norman pulled back with a start and then leaped out of his chair, reached up for a balloon himself, held it close to Jason's face, and then touched it with his cigarette, exploding it. Jason laughed and reached for another balloon. Someone on the other side of the room, caught up in the excitement, pulled a balloon from the ceiling, dropped it to the floor, and stepped on it. And then someone else reached for a balloon, and before any of the dancers realized quite what was happening, the room was resounding with the noise of exploding balloons, and Jason and Norman were laughing hilariously.

"Oh, *get* me one, please," Joan said, "before they break them all. I want to give it to Timmy in the morning."

I reached up for a balloon and pulled it free and handed it to Joan, who began walking toward the bedroom with it, to put it on the bed for safekeeping. But Jason suddenly stepped into her path with a lighted cigarette and he thrust it at the balloon. Joan backed away from him, whirling so that the balloon was out of his reach.

"No!" she said, smiling. "I want this for my son."

But Jason lunged at the balloon again, and Norman came at her from the other side, as if all this explosive action had somehow washed away whatever ill feelings they were harboring, as if they were now united once more in having fun, the thing Jason knew how to lead best, the thing Norman knew how to follow.

"Stop it!" Joan said, holding the balloon high above her head, the smile no longer on her face. I started across the room toward her just as someone turned off the record player and turned on the radio. It was getting close to midnight, and the noise from Times Square was deafening, the announcer shouting over it in an attempt to describe the scene. Joan whirled again, but she was caught by Norman and Jason, who poked at the balloon with their cigarettes as I reached her side.

"Come on . . ." I started to say, and suddenly Jason's cigarette touched the balloon and it exploded in Joan's face, and she said in a small, incredulous voice, "Oh, why'd you do that? I wanted it for my son," and then Jason and Norman danced away from her, reaching up with their cigarettes to burst every balloon in the room, and suddenly the announcer was counting backward, ". . . nine, eight, seven, six, five, four, three, two, one . . ." and there was a pause, and he yelled, "Happy New Year! Happy New Year, everybody! It's a new *year*, everybody!" and the room went silent as we heard the words and turned to our wives.

I took Joan in my arms. I was surprised to feel tears on her face. I kissed her gently, and then I kissed her again, and then I simply held her in my arms and looked around the room where everyone was kissing his wife, and Joan whispered blankly, "I wanted it for Timmy," and suddenly Jason began laughing again and shouting, "Happy New Year! Happy New Year! Happ—"

His voice stopped abruptly. I turned to look at him and saw the grin starting on his face and then followed his gaze to where Herbie, lipstick-smeared, was moving away from Shirley. I smiled because I knew what Herbie was about to do. He was reaching for Mary's hand, and I knew he would kiss her for the new year, a custom we had always followed in my boyhood home, a custom we had followed at adolescent parties and college parties, a custom that so far as I knew was followed everywhere in the world on New Year's Eve, even among young marrieds on North Brother Island. Grinning, Herbie reached over to kiss Mary on the cheek, and she pulled away from him.

I don't think he realized she was ducking his kiss at first. He thought, perhaps, that she didn't understand what he was trying to do, so he reached for her cheek with his lips again, and this time Mary giggled and definitely pulled away from him and said, "Oh, Herbie, *no!*" and I saw the puzzled look cross Herbie's face because he couldn't understand what was quite so objectionable. I had begun to shake my head, ready to tell Mary that all he wanted to do was kiss her for the new year, when suddenly I heard Jason's voice yelling, "Herbie wants to kiss the ladies!" and then Norman shouted, "Go ahead, Herbie, kiss all the ladies!"

Herbie stopped dead in the center of the room.

"Isn't . . ." He shrugged helplessly. "Back home, we . . ." He shrugged again.

"Sure, Herbie," Jason said, "go ahead, kiss them! Kiss them all! Mary, Herbie wants to kiss you!"

"No, that's all right," Herbie said. "You see, back home, it's what we . . ."

"*Kiss* him!" Jason said angrily, and he shoved Mary across the room and into Herbie's arms. Herbie was blushing now, a deep blush that started on his thick neck and worked its way over his face. He kissed Mary on the cheek quickly and then turned with one hand outstretched, embarrassed, reaching for the reassurance of his wife. But Jason yelled again, "That was fun! Kiss them all, Herbie!"

and he grabbed Herbie's outstretched hand and dragged him across the room.

The room was silent now. Jason clung to Herbie's hand and led him from woman to woman as if he were forcing him to run a gauntlet. With each kiss Herbie blushed more furiously. His eyes behind the thick glasses were blinking in confusion, as if he wondered how such a simple thing had suddenly become so monstrous. Beside me, I could feel Joan trembling. I watched in fascinated horror as Jason led Herbie around the room, holding his wrist tightly, shouting, "That was fun! Now the next one!" after each kiss. There were fourteen women besides Shirley in that room. The silence persisted as Herbie kissed each one of them. He turned away from the last woman in a blind sort of panic, searching for Shirley, seeing her, and then rushing across the room as Jason shouted, "How'd you like that, Herbie? You like kissing the girls, huh?"

"*I* like kissing them, too," I said suddenly, surprised when the words came from my mouth. I squeezed Joan's hand quickly and briefly, and then I walked to where Shirley stood against the wall, her eyes frightened and confused, and I said, "Happy New Year, Shirley," and I kissed her gently on the cheek. I went around the silent room wishing each of the women a happy new year, and then I took Joan's hand, and I picked up the container of gin and orange juice, and I walked to the door and without turning I said, "Good night."

In the hallway Joan said, "I love you."

I didn't say anything. I felt as if I'd lost something in that apartment, and I didn't know what the hell it was. We undressed quietly. Before we got into bed, Joan said again, "I love you," and I nodded and turned my head into the pillow.

In a little while I heard the sound coming from the apartment next door. I got out of bed and walked to the wall. The sound was deep and soul-shattering, the sound of a grown man crying.

I stood near the wall listening, and then I bunched my fist and I banged it against the plasterboard, banged it with all my might, and I yelled, "Herbie!" as though I were yelling to a man who was drowning while I stood on the shore.

The sobbing stopped.

There was a silence.

"Yes?" Herbie answered in his thick Midwestern voice.

"Herbie," I yelled, "Happy New Year. You hear me, Herbie? Happy New Year!"

There was another silence.

Then Herbie said, "I hear you."